A SING & SHOUT THRILLER

Strawberry FIELDS

PATRICK D. JOYCE

SPY POND PRESS CAMBRIDGE, MA

Published by Spy Pond Press
125 Mount Auburn St., #380657, Cambridge, MA 02238
www.spypondpress.com
info@spypondpress.com

ISBN 979-8-9861699-3-4 (ebook)
ISBN 979-8-9861699-4-1 (paperback)
ISBN 979-8-9861699-5-8 (hardcover)

This is a work of the imagination in its entirety. All names, settings, incidents, and dialogue have been invented, and when real places, products, and public figures are mentioned in the story, they are used fictionally and without any claim of endorsement or affiliation. Any resemblance between characters in the novel and real people is strictly a coincidence.

Cover design by Damonza.com
Spy Pond Press logo design by Priya K. Joyce
Interior LP record image by JeksonGraphics/Shutterstock.com

Library of Congress Control Number: 2024900191

24061107

If you enjoy this book, visit patrickdjoyce.com, where you can sign up for author updates and receive a free short story.

For Rajee

*Down went Alice after it, never once considering
how in the world she was to get out again.*

Lewis Carroll

*From a certain point there is no more turning back.
That is the point that must be reached.*

Franz Kafka

Side One

THE BRIDGE

Just before dawn a mist crept across the Charles Bridge. It slid over the cobblestones and climbed up the lampposts. The heavy sky pressed down upon Prague, but the city pushed back with its steeples and monuments. The world seemed not quite real.

Statues lined the bridge, thirty dead saints. In the daylight they wore varied expressions, but at this hour they all gazed blankly downward, watching and waiting for a passerby who might tip the balance of history in their favor.

On this August morning in 1968, a young woman walked onto the bridge, touching the feet of the saints as she went. The mist curled at her heels, like it was trying to discover who she was and what she was doing, all alone at this early hour.

She peered into the gloom. She was looking for someone.

In spite of all her efforts to get to this moment, she felt a temptation to turn back. She'd arouse suspicion if she waited too long. Her source had named this time and place, and he hadn't showed up. Maybe he'd run into trouble. Maybe he'd been arrested.

Her doubts gathered and transformed into ugly shapes. They flew back at her and perched on her shoulders like gargoyles.

As if to join them, a cloud separated from the mist ahead and condensed into a figure. A man. Like the air itself had produced him, like the progression of matter through its states. Gas, liquid, solid. Mist, dew, man.

He drew closer and details appeared, but not many. The folds of a woolen scarf hid his face. A brimmed hat hooded his eyes, casting them in shadow.

The young woman kept her attention forward as she reached into her shoulder bag. She pulled out a pen and notepad, her sword and shield. If this meeting went right, they would save her. If it went wrong, would they spell her doom?

Her name was Josie Brouk, and she was a correspondent for the *Toronto Post*. She was new to Prague. It was her first posting abroad, and the job had not been easy. She had struggled to learn the pitfalls of reporting inside a communist state. She had picked up bits of wisdom here and there, following the lead of other Western journalists. Sometimes they bothered to notice her as they milled outside the National Assembly. Sometimes they did not.

But Josie had a skill most of them lacked. She spoke Czech. She'd learned it from her grandmother. Most of her family had dropped their traditions after they'd arrived in Canada, before Josie was born, but her babička had kept them all, language included. She'd made Josie her collaborator in preserving the old ways. Josie, as she'd grown up, was more than willing.

Most of the world saw little value in the country's languages and culture. The great powers saw Czechoslovakia as a bargaining chip, a stepping stone, a distraction that allowed them to engage in geopolitical sleights of hand elsewhere. It came to this: It was a pretty nation with a quaint architecture and storied history, but its future was not its own. Generations of Czechs and Slovaks had fought against that notion, but its fate always seemed to lie in the hands of others. Like the Soviets, who had imprisoned it behind an Iron Curtain.

For Josie, the language of her grandmother opened doors. On the steps of the Assembly, she stood in the path of government officials parading up and down and surprised them with her fluency. It got her the attention she craved, and details other reporters missed. But it didn't get her the stories she needed. As soon as officials talked, the rest of the foreign correspondents circled in, pens at the ready. They couldn't speak fluent Czech, but they had connections, drive, and experience. Some had interpreters or fixers. Josie was new to the scene, alone in her paper's small bureau, and a young woman, forced to prove herself at every turn.

She worried she would lose her job in this place she'd always dreamed about. But she suffered past her mistakes. She struggled through the obstacles. She learned from them.

Josie knew she had to make a splash. She had to deliver a big story to her editors, one nobody else could tell. This meeting with the mysterious source who had summoned her to the bridge felt like that chance. The slip of paper had appeared under her apartment door the night before and told her to come alone. Why? Maybe it wasn't only her last chance. Maybe it was his, too. Or his country's.

Was he alone as well? Would there be others, across the bridge, beyond the fog, hiding in alleys on either side?

If she proceeded to the middle of the bridge, she would be exposed, equidistant from either bank. It was a long bridge. What if it was a trap? Should she go on? Could she find the courage?

She thought of her babička. The stories she'd told Josie were the reason she was here, in this city, on this bridge. Her parents had warned her: *Don't go back there*. But she'd never been there before. How could she go back?

She needed to prove she'd been right. For her babička. For herself.

She walked forward.

A foghorn cut through the haze. It echoed the note of a familiar song, one that Josie could not place. The moment felt like a turning point, and the music of the city magnified the effect. She remembered the simple poetry her babička had often scratched for her, in notes she'd hidden in lunches packed for school. They had inspired Josie to write herself, and later to become a writer. In school, she had learned that words could change the course of history. At some level, she knew hers could too, and someday they would.

The Shrouded Man had said so himself in his note. Its message made her think of her babička.

She held the memory close. She let the foghorn's music pulse in her ears. The energy propelled her forward.

When she was close enough, the Shrouded Man whispered through his scarf.

"You are Canadian, yes?"

He spoke in Czech and was out of breath. He'd been running recently.

"I am," she said.

"You are young."

She coughed. She was nineteen. She'd quit college to take a job at the *Star*. She'd started with trivial stories, dreaming of bigger ones. She filled in for someone on the crime beat, and they let her stay. To the cops, she had seemed meek at first, and they had treated her with indifference, but she was dogged in her work and they quickly lost their illusions. Her persistence became well-known.

Then a public uprising halfway around the world sent its echoes back to Canada, and her editors discovered she spoke Czech. So they sent her.

"That is good," the Shrouded Man said. "Freedom hangs in the balance, for all of us, young and old alike."

His words were clipped. He struggled with them. He opened his mouth to say more, but a noise pierced the sky, more urgent than the foghorn. It was a high-pitched whine, two notes alternating and repeating.

It was a sound meant to reassure, to alert people help was on the way. Often, it did. But here, now, it signaled danger.

It was a siren.

The mist disappeared. The first rays of the rising sun shot over the bridge. The sound of running feet slapped at the stone.

Until that point, the Shrouded Man had moved like the mist around him, slow and deliberate. Now he spun in place. His eyes, visible suddenly in the trench between his hat and his scarf, filled with fear. They frightened Josie.

Men in pale green uniforms appeared at the towers on both sides. They wielded heavy batons. Beyond them, blue lights spun and flashed on the tops of little cars.

They were the VB — the regular public security force of the Czechoslovak Socialist Republic.

A barrage of shouts burst across the bridge, followed by a shrill whistle. From a distance, a cacophony of violent noises broke out. The ground itself seemed to rumble and transmit vibrations through the stone, like a great trouble broadcast from afar.

The Shrouded Man pulled his scarf tight. Josie knew he was about to run. She knew she should run too, even if there was little chance of escape.

It was the rational thing to do.

But sometimes, the irrational thing made more sense.

Josie grabbed his wrist.

"Wait," she said. "Tell me what you came for."

His eyes darted back and forth. He made a quick calculation. In English, he rasped, "I am the walrus."

Josie stared, uncomprehending.

"Sorry, you're ... what?"

"Go to the Café Skrýš. Listen. The Playwright will understand. Trust no one else!"

The words came so fast, between labored puffs, that Josie thought she must have heard him wrong. Another whistle shook the air. The Shrouded Man pulled away. Quicker than seemed possible, he pounced toward the low stone wall and crouched under a saint. For a moment, its shadow concealed him.

Police closed in from both sides of the bridge, seconds away from colliding at the spot where Josie stood. The unfolding events took her by surprise, but they didn't paralyze her. She tucked her pen and notepad into her bag. They'd be no use now, not yet.

She raised her hands, palms forward to show they were empty, but stood her ground.

The Shrouded Man made a different choice. He leaped onto the wall. He took a saint's arm.

Josie gasped.

The VB shouted.

Another whistle blew.

The Shrouded Man jumped.

The impact made a great sucking whoosh. Josie rushed to the edge and looked down. He was gone. His scarf and hat floated on the surface of the water, arranged like symbols in a secret code.

The VB halted at the wall, stumbling into each other. One jumped in after the Shrouded Man. One pointed at the opposite bank. Another rushed there, aiming to intercept him.

THE TANKS

The squad car radio blared. From the back seat, Josie recognized the song: its fanfare of trumpets, a blast of rhythmic psychedelic sound — "Magical Mystery Tour," the Beatles song from the album of the same name. They sang it like ringmasters in a circus of insanity. In sync with the music, the squad car careened through the narrow streets like it had lost control.

The song itself was a sign of how much the Prague Spring movement had lit a fire.

Before the reforms, barely four months ago, you never heard Western music on the radio, only on foreign broadcasts that managed to penetrate the Iron Curtain. Now the local stations played Beatles songs and all kinds of Western rock and pop as much as they liked. Popular American and British bands had even come to perform public concerts. On top of that, music from the West was finding its way out of Prague through underground routes into the neighboring communist states where it was still banned — even into the Soviet Union itself.

The world was taking notice.

Decades ago, Nazi Germany had overrun Czechoslovakia without a second thought. The great powers of Europe had left it out of the Munich Agreement that had preceded the shocking invasion. Afterward, they barely blinked an eye, and events overwhelmed the people of the small nation. Destiny, it seemed, had sucked them under.

This time, the people of Czechoslovakia made the first move. Instead of letting others decide the course of history, they decided to make it themselves.

The end of World War II had locked them inside the Soviet Union's sphere of influence, but writers and artists had begun to challenge the restrictions on expression. A brave new leader, Alexander Dubček, heard the call for reforms and channeled the new spirit. In January, he won elections to become First Secretary of the Communist Party. He promised to establish new policies of openness — and even a measure of freedom. He called it "socialism with a human face."

People poked their heads out of hiding places, and the movement gained momentum. They expressed themselves in the newspapers, in magazines, on the radio, on street corners, in cafés. Popular support for Dubček and his reforms was overwhelming.

Hope bloomed. The world over, it became known as the Prague Spring.

But corners of darkness remained. Uncertainties loomed. This fight was a story whose ending had not been written.

Josie knew Dubček's reforms were popular, but she knew he had enemies too. Hard-liners opposed it. Conflicts were brewing, tensions mounting. And no one knew how much the Soviet overlords would tolerate.

She knew that whatever the Shrouded Man had meant to tell her, he'd placed himself in grave danger. But she also knew he must have arranged the meeting because he had no choice.

Now Josie was at the mercy of the VB. They hadn't cuffed her, but the cramped back seat offered nothing to hold on to and she hit the doors every time the squad car swerved. The Old Town was all tight corners. Architects in the Middle Ages had designed it like a maze. Certainly they hadn't meant it as a racetrack.

She peppered the officers with questions, but they refused to answer. They had taken her into custody without explanation. Then they'd taken her press card. Now she thrust her passport at them. The one in the passenger seat grabbed it and examined it. They acted like they were doing her a favor, taking her somewhere she needed to be.

She tried to read their faces, discern what lay behind the feline grins. Suddenly their smiles dropped. Their jaws hung loose. The car slowed.

The panorama was unreal. A parade of tanks crawled down the long boulevard. Helmeted soldiers poked out of turrets. Clumps of bystanders, halted on their ways to work, gawked in disbelief.

Josies searched the tanks for markings.

"Your armed forces don't have that kind of artillery," she said. "Where'd they come from?"

She didn't pose the question for an answer. She was thinking aloud. She knew the tanks could only come from one place. A part of her hoped the officers wouldn't respond, because they would have to give her the answer she dreaded. But the driver decided to speak. Maybe he was thinking aloud too.

"I ... I don't know."

The other officer swiveled to face her. "You are a journalist. You tell us."

They fell silent.

The tanks bore no flags. No signs to identify their nationality. Only numbers stenciled on the sides, and white stripes painted in thick lines across the top like crosses.

She knew where the tanks came from. Did they really not? Could they deny it?

Josie studied their eyes in the rearview mirror and read a single emotion: shock. They were helpless. A force greater than theirs possessed the streets.

Her dread dissipated. A thrill replaced it. Josie forgot about her failures and insecurities. She forgot about the Shrouded Man and the bridge. The Soviets had sent troops into Prague, and she was smack in the middle of an invasion. The foreign news bureaus had yet to open. The reporters who had ignored her for months lay asleep in their beds. This was the story she'd been waiting for.

She leaned forward and shouted at the officers. "Can you move faster? I have to get to my office. I have to call my newspaper. There! Turn there."

But they were mesmerized and once again ignored her.

The *Toronto Post*'s bureau in Prague consisted of a room in a suite with a single phone shared by five other papers. Unless she got there fast, she would lose her chance at the phone. A reporter would be on the line already, with more queued up.

"No. Wait. Stop here. Anywhere. I need a public phone."

They stopped the car.

Josie grinned. Maybe she sounded more commanding than she realized.

"One phone call. I'll come right back."

Josie grabbed the door handle. To her surprise, it was loose. If she kept jiggling, she might be able to force it open.

Then she saw why they'd stopped. A little yellow Fiat had entered the street, blocking the way. The man at the wheel was panicked. He struggled with his door. He hadn't turned fast enough. It was a sad mistake.

A mountain on treads advanced toward him. He rolled down his window, but it was too late. The tank barreled onto the front of the car, crushing it. A scream and a metal crunch erupted outside. The windshield shattered, spraying shards of glass onto the man inside. The tank continued down the avenue.

Josie's thrill turned to horror. She knew the tank had just cost the man his legs, possibly his life.

A woman passing near the Fiat wailed. Shouts rose from people down the street. But their voices only accentuated the sense that all usual sounds had been smothered. One man dropped to his knees, wordless. Everyone else stood still, stunned and confused.

Behind the tanks came flatbed trucks with low rails carrying dozens of soldiers. Their mouths made grim lines. They held rifles raised at oblique angles.

The police officers recovered. In the confusion, their sense of duty was all they had, and it saved them. They backed up and turned down a side street.

Josie settled back into her seat. She cursed the Soviet troops, the Czech police, and her own bad luck. On the radio, "Magical Mystery Tour" neared its end. The tempo slowed and the raucous carnival died away, replaced by a series of ominous piano keys that jumped up and down the scale, wavering at points, until the music faded out.

THE CELL

The squad car skidded to a stop alongside a building whose facade was covered in gray tiles and opaque windows. A heavy arch and faux columns framed the entryway. Josie knew what it was. The place was infamous. People who went in there were swallowed up and never heard from again.

This was Bartolomějská Street. Police headquarters.

The officers seemed dazed as they pulled Josie out of the back seat. The daylight had grown. In the distance, curls of smoke rose above the buildings. The city was too quiet.

They had her by the arms. As they entered the station, she wriggled, and they released her. She had nowhere to run. But more than that, they had lost all expression. Like they had been hollowed out.

Another officer behind a desk stopped them and pointed to a ledger. One took a pen and scribbled. The others engaged in hurried conversation.

A heavy door to the side opened, and yet another officer beckoned. The first two motioned her to walk through, and she found herself in a long corridor full of doors. Some were open, some closed. The officer chose a closed one at the end. He pushed it open and thrust her through. It slammed behind her.

The small room contained a bench and a chair. The single window was high and crisscrossed with bars. She smoothed her skirt, sat on the bench, and took out her notebook. She wrote down all the details she could remember. Not from the bridge — after. The suddenness of the tanks, their cryptic white markings, the soldiers' expressions like ghosts, the shock and confusion among the people on the streets.

She didn't dare describe the Shrouded Man. Not on paper. Not here. Maybe not anytime, anywhere.

Josie thought about the day her editors had told her they wanted to send her to Prague. She'd been thrilled, elated, and shocked. She wanted the job. It was her dream come true.

Never in a million years could she have guessed she would find herself in a jail cell. In the middle of an undeclared war. Up until a few hours ago her life had seemed like one great big adventure. Even with all the challenges she faced, she'd felt like she was playing at a game.

Now she'd stepped into a different world. A world that was suddenly more adult, more real — and more dangerous.

A clanging came from the hall. The door opened. Josie tried to thrust the notepad into her bag but fumbled. The bag dropped to the floor. Her pen flew across the dirty linoleum, hitting the door in mid-swing, and ricocheted to the side.

A tall figure entered, carrying a ring of keys and a clipboard, and pulled the door shut behind her. She wore her hair pulled back and sported a nose like an axe blade. She had stars on the shoulder of her uniform and medals on her chest. A commander. But the surest sign of her power wasn't the decorations. It was the calm severity of her presence and the unbroken line of her lips.

She flipped through a set of papers on the clipboard. Josie waited, then lost her patience.

"What's happening out there? Are you taking orders from Soviet forces now? Where's the Czechoslovak army? What —"

"Quiet! I will ask the questions." The Commander's voice made the cell — and Josie — tremble.

Josie felt muted, like she'd lost control of her vocal cords.

"You are Josefina Brouková?"

The Commander had attached Czech's traditional feminine ending to her surname. Josie had grown up without it in Canada, but she'd grown accustomed to using it here. It was expected.

"That's right."

"What were you doing on the Charles Bridge?"

"Taking a morning stroll. Listen, I have to —"

"That is a lie. Do you want to spend the rest of the day in this cell? While the world changes outside?"

"I'm a Canadian citizen and a journalist. You have no right to detain me. I have to get to a phone."

"You and the rest of the foreign press are to blame for what is happening. You have spread dangerous temptations to the people of my country. Prague newspapers and radio, writers and artists, have gone too far. Look at the result."

The Commander paused, regained her cool, and proceeded.

"Even journalists must abide by the law," she continued. "You have consorted with a criminal. I can show mercy, but you must give me what I need."

What she *needs*, Josie thought. Not what she *wants*. Someone higher up has issued orders. The VB were regular police. They attended to public order, traffic and criminal duties. It was the StB that handled State Security. It comprised a smaller force, but it was far more powerful. Sometimes they clashed. The StB always won.

Josie had arrived in a VB car. But who was this interrogating her? And under what orders?

"All I want to do is make one phone call. Then I'm happy to talk about what you need. I'll tell you all about my stroll across your beautiful city."

"I know someone contacted you. You met him on the bridge. I need to know his name."

"I don't know his name."

"Now we are getting somewhere. How did he contact you?"

Josie knew she had to give up something if she was to get out of here.

"He slipped a note under my door."

"What did he say to you?"

"Nothing. He didn't have time. Your goons spooked him. He jumped off the bridge."

That was the important part. Josie had to lie convincingly.

The Commander leaned in. She filled Josie's entire field of vision. Her large features appeared warped in close-up, as if magnified by a giant lens.

"I do not want to be here with you any more than you want to be here with me. As I see it, you are wasting my time. Why have I been ordered to detain a young woman, barely out of her teens, who looks as innocent as she pretends, while tanks crush my city? While thousands more line the highways? While my country falls to pieces?"

She leaned in even closer.

"Who are you, Josefina Brouková? What do you know?"

Josie gulped.

For a moment, she thought to tell the Commander what the Shrouded Man had said before jumping. *I am the walrus.* To spite her. Because the words made no sense. He was the walrus? What did it mean?

Of course, Josie had recognized the words. "I Am the Walrus" was the fiercely nonsensical track on *Magical Mystery Tour*. She knew the album well. She'd bought the LP in Toronto a month before leaving for Prague, had listened to it over and over. The Shrouded Man had to be referring to the song. What else could he mean? And he'd commented on her age — as if to confirm she'd know the music.

But what did a Beatles song have to do with anything? With freedom? With the course of history? Was he referring to himself? What made *him* the Walrus?

The Shrouded Man could have said a hundred other things before diving off the bridge. But he believed he'd been in danger. He'd been right. And he possessed information that was so important he'd risked his life for it. So what had he meant?

She recalled the song. Its organ-grinder quality, the made up-sounding words, the rising chorus, the mysterious voices in the background, some of them chanting, some reciting lines from a radio play that had aired on the BBC, which the Beatles had captured for random effect.

She remembered the first time she'd heard it. None of it made sense. But it wound her up. The more she listened to the song, the more it had come together and taken on a meaning and feeling greater than the sum of any of its words or sounds. It seethed with power, and bewilderment, and frustration. It was brilliant.

But now she could only imagine the Shrouded Man had been delirious. Or crazy.

She cursed her luck again. Another worthless lead, another failure in a long string. And now the police had driven her straight through an invasion — the biggest story in Prague's recent history, possibly the biggest in the world right now and certainly the biggest in her own career. But she'd ended up in a cell. A cell they might hold her in for hours.

The Commander looked Josie up and down, then spoke.

"You are not under arrest. Go make your phone call. Take your time and use it wisely. You are a smart girl. Reconsider your reticence. Come back here before the end of the day and give me a name. Then I will be happy, because the people who consider you a threat will get what they want."

Josie stood up.

"There's just one thing. The officers who brought me here —"

"You are wondering about these?"

The Commander flashed a booklet and a badge. Josie's passport and press card, which the police in the squad car had taken from her.

"Yes, thank you."

Josie reached out. The Commander drew back.

"They stay with me."

"What? No!"

"Then?"

"I told you! I don't know who he is."

Josie's heart pounded. She hoped her interrogator would believe her.

"Without your papers, you are nothing but a girl who speaks Czech in the middle of an invasion of a country you cannot leave. Pray you are not asked for papers by anyone who speaks Russian." The Commander tapped her temple. "But I think your memory will improve. When it does, I will give your papers back."

The Commander rose and stomped her foot to turn, military style. She knocked once and barked an order. The cell door opened, and the Commander walked out.

She left the door open.

The People

Josie jumped to her feet and went for the cell door. She'd almost crossed the threshold when she remembered her pen.

She returned to the cell, pulled the door wide, and retrieved it. Stuffing it back into her shoulder bag, she peeked out. A flurry of activity filled the corridor, police officers and clerks crisscrossing on either side. She stepped out. No one stopped her. She recognized one of the officers from the squad car. He glanced at her blankly before continuing down the corridor.

The Commander had disappeared.

Did they expect her to stay? To give them a name? And if she stayed, would they give back her papers?

But she couldn't. Every minute that passed inside this walled sanctuary, or fortress, or prison, was an opportunity lost.

She marched back to the front and pleaded in Czech with the desk officer. She told him she'd been deprived of her papers and demanded them back. He responded with a stony expression and went about his business.

Josie fumed and reverted to English. "I'm foreign press. You can't do this to me."

"You say you're press? Prove it."

"I can't. You have my papers. That's what I'm trying to tell you."

"A likely story."

"Can you at least tell me where to find the Commander who questioned me?"

"Who?"

"She was scary. She had lots of medals."

"Commander Tesařová?"

A phone on the desk rang, and the officer picked it up. Josie wanted to scream. She grunted instead, and stamped her foot.

A voice came from behind her.

"Excuse me, are you all right?"

Josie turned to see a young man carrying a notepad and a pen. He had a press badge on his lapel. He wore a beige linen suit that hung smartly on his lanky frame, the fit making it look more expensive than it probably was.

"I overheard. Is something wrong?"

He spoke English with a slight accent. Josie couldn't place it. He wasn't Canadian or American. African, she thought, or European.

"Yes, something is wrong," she said. "They questioned me, took something of mine, and now they won't give it back."

"They interrogated you, and they let you go?"

Josie, preoccupied with her papers, thought it was a strange question.

"How do you know I was interrogated? Maybe I was reporting a burglary."

"Today? I don't think so. I don't know what happened in there. But I know it couldn't have been easy. I'm only trying to help."

Josie realized she was shaking. A siren rang through the air. Muffled thuds echoed in the distance.

"I'm sorry. You're kind. I appreciate your concern, but it isn't necessary. I have to get to a phone."

"You can't trust them, you know. If they want information from you, they won't stand around waiting for it. Have you been in Prague long? The police here —"

Josie swung around. She could tell he meant well, but the implication that she lacked experience incensed her, even if it was true. Deeper down, she was embarrassed. She was afraid the predicament reflected her own failings.

"I'm not naive. I can handle myself."

"I just mean they have ways to intimidate you. They know how to get what they want."

"They've already done that. They took my papers."

"Oh dear."

"I was at the river meeting a source and the police came and took me, and now I'm here and I still haven't called my editors. I have to go. Thanks for your concern, but I'll figure this out myself."

He lowered his voice to a whisper. "They let you go so they could follow you. They want you to lead them to your source."

Josie gasped. She hadn't considered that. The encounter with the Shrouded Man and everything after it had rattled her.

"If they think that's going to work, good luck to them. I don't know who he is, or where he is, or how to find him."

"Be careful. You don't —"

"No one's going to follow me. Not this time."

Josie burst through the door and left the police station.

"Wait. What's your name? What paper do you write for?"

Josie felt herself tear up. She was angry — at the police, at her source, at herself. She knew she was being unfair, taking it out on the nice man, who was young like she was and a reporter too. Why did she feel like she was making a mistake, walking away? Like she should be trusting him?

Yet Josie picked up her pace. Let the police follow. She had to focus on the task before her. She had to get to a phone. She had to call in the story.

Josie set out to find a commercial avenue where she could find a public phone or a shop that had one.

As she searched, she absorbed details of the scene surrounding her. She counted the tanks and the jeeps and the other Soviet machinery. She made columns and lists in her notepad. She scribbled descriptions.

As the streets around her filled with armored vehicles, her attention drifted back to the police station. A moment from the interrogation stuck in her mind. She'd dropped her bag, with her notepad in plain view, but the Commander had ignored it. She hadn't picked it up, or even asked for it. She made no attempt to rifle through it. Of course, Josie hadn't written anything about the Shrouded Man, but the Commander didn't know that. She could have taken it, but she hadn't.

Josie thought about the other journalist. Was he right? But why would the police care about her, or even the Shrouded Man, in the middle of an invasion? She almost couldn't blame the Commander. Josie wanted answers too.

She scanned the scene around her. People were still confused, but the shock was wearing off. Men in summer suits and women in light frocks held brick-sized portable radios to their ears. Their faces contorted in anger. A few brave souls walked up to the tanks and accosted the Soviet soldiers.

A woman with dark curls and a camera strap around her neck approached Josie. She took her hand and placed a small object in her palm.

It was a roll of film. Josie understood right away. The woman had seen her writing notes, knew she was a reporter, and recognized her as a foreigner. She wanted Josie to take her photos out of the country and make sure they appeared in a newspaper or magazine.

The woman ran off down an alley. The opening at the other end revealed a new column of heavy trucks rolling past.

The incident pierced Josie's very identity. The simple act by a woman she had never met lent her a powerful sense of belonging, not because she was in any way special, but because everyone here had a role to perform. Like it or not, history had cast them in a play whose ending she hoped had not yet been written.

It made her feel important. But it also gave her a burden — a responsibility, not only to the *Post*, but to these people who were not quite her own.

Josie tucked the roll of film into her pocket and approached a man nearby who stood wide-eyed on the sidewalk. Behind him an overturned cart spilled red onto the street. Not blood — not yet. Ripe strawberries. Farms outside Prague grew them. The countryside here was famous for them. But they were out of season now, and she was surprised to see them. These were crushed, leaking their juice.

"Excuse me. Do you know where I can find a phone?"

He didn't answer. She put her hand on his shoulder and shook him gently.

"Please. I need a phone."

"What? The tobacconist, over there. He has a phone."

His lips moved, but Josie could tell he barely registered she was there. He was fixated on the moving columns and the stone-faced soldiers. He might need help. She'd tell the tobacconist.

"Thank you," she said, and she started toward the shop he'd indicated.

But she stopped at the curb and nearly fell into the street.

A tank halted there. Soldiers with puffy cheeks and intense expressions clambered up onto the armored plates. Two soldiers already riding on top, Josie's age or younger, gave them a hand up. They'd been running. Soviet forces owned Prague now. Yet the soldiers on the sidewalk looked anxious.

She saw why.

A crowd clustered around the tank. They were young too. The girls wore miniskirts, and the boys sported blue jeans and Beatles haircuts. They carried satchels and books. Josie saw a sign two blocks down: *Radio Prague*. It was where the tanks were headed. The students had run after the soldiers and begun to line up in front of the radio station. The armed troops facing them looked distinctly uncomfortable.

To move forward, the tank would have to barrel through them. The soldiers sweated under their padded helmets. Another tank approached behind it, then another, and another.

None of the students budged. Beyond them, in front of the radio station, vehicles formed a barricade: bakery trucks, streetcars, a fire engine. Josie braced herself. Either the tank would plow forward in complete disregard for human life, or it would sit there for a long time, stymied.

Josie couldn't say which would happen. All she knew was she could no longer cross the street safely. The students hemmed her in from behind as well. The crowd expanded.

A Czechoslovak flag, white, red, and blue, was thrust upward over the restless mass. Voices cried out and grew louder. The students chanted. Objects flew through the air. An apple traced a graceful arc and exploded on a turret. A heavy book hit a soldier in the head. Someone lit a folded newspaper on fire and tossed it onto the tank, which caught fire. Flames licked at the back of other tanks as they moved down the street. The smell of burning rubber was everywhere. Soldiers jumped down from another tank and beat the flames with blankets. Another shouted into a walkie-talkie.

Shots rang out — soldiers had fired into the air. The crowd frenzied before the tanks, and a path opened through the middle. Josie took a chance and ran through the opening, across the street. The tanks moved forward, dragging flames, crushing trees on the sidewalks, mangling cars. The crowds condensed around them again.

Josie pushed through the tobacco shop's glass door. The establishment was empty, with the exception of the tobacconist himself. He had a mustache, wire glasses, and sparse hair. He stood behind the counter absorbed with the radio, which crackled with energy.

"The invading forces are in control of the airport," a voice said. "Here at Radio Prague, they have surrounded the building."

Machine-gun fire rattled in the distance. On the radio, it grew louder, like someone had dropped a mic out a window.

"They have entered the building! We stand behind Dubček! We will never give up!"

Then silence, and static.

"Please, sir, can I use your phone?"

The tobacconist fiddled with a dial on the radio and pointed absentmindedly to a shelf at the end of the counter, where the telephone sat, its plastic dial gleaming below a lamp.

Josie rushed over and lifted the handset. The rotary stuck and her fingers felt numb, so she redialed twice before she got the operator. She gave the number for the *Post* in Toronto and asked to reverse the charges.

The voice of the operator sounded surreal in its calmness. The woman had to be somewhere in Prague. Did she know what was going on? What about the rest of the world? Did they know?

Josie reminded herself: that was *her* job. To make it known.

A male voice answered. "*Toronto Post* news desk."

"Sam? It's Josie. Are you at a typewriter?"

"Josie? What's going on?"

"This is big. Are you ready?"

"Hold on."

Josie heard a clunk, like Sam had dropped the handset. Sam's voice: "Ow! Damn." Shuffling noises.

"Spilled a hot coffee. Okay, I'm ready."

"Here goes." Josie cleared her throat. "Soviet tanks thundered into Prague this morning, taking the city by surprise and the world by storm ..."

THE SLAVIA

Josie considered going home, back to her one-room apartment above the flower shop in Malá Strana. She could take a minute, regroup, and plan her next steps. Sam had put an editor on the phone, and he'd given her pointers on what to do next. He told her to call with another update in the afternoon.

She said nothing about the Shrouded Man or her encounter with the police. She didn't need pity or scolding or doubts.

But after the call, a single idea dominated Josie's thoughts. She wanted to find the café the Shrouded Man had told her about.

She saw two possibilities. First, she might find herself in the middle of a story that was bigger than she could imagine. The timing of the Shrouded Man's secret appeal the night before and then their meeting on the bridge, right as Soviet forces were entering Prague, made her certain. They were connected.

The second, less palatable, was that she could find information to give the police commander. If it came to that, it would have to be good enough to get her papers back, but without endangering anyone's life. Like the first possibility, it was difficult to imagine.

Did it have to be one or the other? She hoped not. She wanted a story, and she wanted her papers back.

What had he said? *Go to the Café Skrýš.*

Prague was known for its coffeehouses. Legendary writers and intellectuals and students had gathered in them for time out of mind. They debated. They created. The city had dozens of coffeehouses, each historic and unique in its own way. The Café Louvre, for instance, where Franz Kafka had spun his weird tales and Albert Einstein his even weirder theories.

But the heart of the city's coffee culture today had to be the Art Deco–style Café Slavia on Národní Street. Like the others, it had an illustrious past. The beloved poet and novelist Rainer Maria Rilke had sipped coffee there, watching the River Vltava drift past the plate glass windows. He'd used the place as a setting for his stories.

But the Slavia was different from other coffeehouses not because of its past but because of what was happening there in the present. More than the rest, it married literature and ideas with politics. Its patrons were interested in art and beauty and philosophy, but they also wanted to change the world. To make it better.

What else had the Shrouded Man said? *The Playwright will understand.* It meant the Café Skrýš served writers too. Perhaps in a way the Slavia didn't, or couldn't.

Josie had never heard of it. But if it existed, someone at the Slavia would know about it.

Josie pushed through lines of protesters, street after street, until she found herself at the Slavia. The place was packed, and it was thick with the aroma of coffee. Customers adorned with goatees and berets conversed with an animation that rivaled the energy on the streets. Strident arguments battled the sounds of cups clattering against saucers. Men twirled index fingers in a cigarette smoke–tinged haze that hung low beneath ornate chandeliers.

She heard snippets of conversation about the Soviet troops and the Czechoslovak government. She heard Alexander Dubček's name, in anger, in concern. He'd disappeared. Was he dead? Arrested? Or had he fled? Had he betrayed his own people?

She tried to catch a waiter's attention. There were several, weaving through the tables, focused on their jobs. So focused they paid her no attention — it was as if she didn't exist. A man with scraggly hair and a long beard tapped her on the shoulder.

"You need a table first," he advised.

Every table was taken, but some had open chairs. Josie made for the nearest one, occupied by old men gesticulating animatedly, and touched the chair back as if to claim it. She parted her lips, about to speak, when a voice called out in English.

"Hello!"

Someone was waving at her.

Through all the talking heads and flailing arms, a man sat at a small table, alone with a pen and notepad. Josie wondered why she hadn't noticed him right away. His unassuming figure seemed to blend in, hiding in plain sight. He raised his cup.

The journalist from the police station.

She had one mission, one question to answer. She didn't have time to socialize, to fend him off again, no matter how well-intentioned he was. But he didn't have the time either. What was he doing here? Perhaps there was more than one question to be answered in this place.

It wouldn't hurt to join him for a few minutes. They could compare notes.

He'd been scribbling. As she sat down, he welcomed her and glanced at his watch. He's meeting someone, she thought.

Someone who's late. Or someone who stood him up. She felt a pang of sympathy.

A waiter appeared. She ordered a coffee.

"The *Toronto Post.*"

"Pardon?"

"The paper I write for. You asked back at the police station."

"Oh, of course. I'm with *Paris Flash.* Laurent Akobo. Nice to meet you."

"Josie Brouk. You're French? I couldn't tell."

"I'm good with accents. As a boy I mimicked everything I heard. Birds, people, music."

"In France?"

"In Ethiopia. I attended a French school in Addis Ababa, then studied in Paris. I stayed there when civil strife overcame my home."

He was young, like her. He couldn't be more than a year or two older.

"Was it hard, leaving your family? Adapting to a new home?"

"It was. My parents died when I was a boy, but I had aunts and uncles and cousins, who I haven't seen since. And Paris has its challenges, but it's what I wanted to do."

"My grandparents left their home too, after the First World War. They lived in a village outside Prague. They never came back."

"So that's why you speak Czech."

"How did you —?"

"When you ordered."

"Oh. Sometimes I don't notice I'm speaking it. I learned it when I was little, from my grandmother. She spoke to me in Czech. She refused to speak English. And she refused to forget the old country. She told me stories, about the strawberry farm where she played as a child, about the village where she grew up, about my grandfather, a tailor, whom I never met. About the war, and the pain it caused her family. I was happy to be her coconspirator. Czech was our secret code."

"You must have loved her a great deal. Her language was a gift."

"Yes." She might have judged this man too quickly. He was interesting, and thoughtful. "Yes, it was."

"It must be useful now."

"It's why the *Post* sent me."

"And what are you doing here?"

"In Czechoslovakia?"

He laughed. "In the Slavia."

"I might ask you the same."

"Except I asked you first."

"Can't I be here for a cup of coffee? I think I deserve it."

"Touché."

His curiosity seemed genuine. Josie looked straight in his eyes. She could tell it made him uncomfortable, but she didn't stop. He seemed confident, but not excessively. She liked that she could unnerve him.

Suddenly, he leaned in close.

"I've been worried about you since the police station. Why were they so interested in you? I know it was the VB that picked you up, but there could be more to it. Others involved."

"Right now, with the Soviet army about to occupy the city, I'm sure there's interest in every foreign journalist. You included."

"That's just it. They don't seem much concerned about us. Not the Czechoslovaks in charge, nor the Soviets either. They did cut power to hotels this morning, including my bureau's, but that's all. They're obsessed with the local press, like they have been all year. Have you heard about Radio Prague?"

"I saw it. It's frightening."

The young man's sincerity intrigued her, but she began to feel her burden. She sipped her coffee. Out the broad windows, the many bridges of Prague spanned the Vltava. The Charles Bridge wasn't far. The statues of the saints looked tiny from here, not the impressive figures they'd appeared up close. But the Shrouded Man loomed large in her mind.

"The source you met, the one police questioned you about. Who was he?"

He seemed to know what she was thinking.

"Like I told them, I don't know. He sent a note last night saying he had important information to give me. Today the timing makes it seem like it was related to the invasion."

"So he wasn't able to give you the information?"

"No, unfortunately." Josie bit her lip. She liked him, but she had to be careful. "Your turn. What were you doing at police headquarters?"

"I was looking for someone. A party official I know."

"Why aren't you out there now, reporting on the tanks?"

"My colleagues are on that. I've been assigned another task. I might get a few sentences in the main story, but no byline of my own. I tend to get the assignments no one else wants. I suppose I should be grateful to be here at all. The editor is an old friend of my university advisor. I finished my coursework in half the time, and he persuaded the editor I was worth a risk."

"What's the task they assigned you?"

Josie was curious. Her impatience to get on with her mission faded. She watched him perk up, like he hadn't expected anyone to take an interest in his assignment.

"A letter was published this morning in newspapers across the communist bloc. It claimed to be written by Czechoslovak party officials, sent to the Kremlin. It decried the reforms of the Prague Spring, said they've gone too far, and invited Soviet troops into the country. To establish order."

"That's ridiculous. Who did the newspapers say wrote the letter?"

"They didn't. The letter was unsigned. So everyone assumes it's a fiction, made up by the Soviets to justify their actions."

"But your editor wants you to get the official reactions. All bound to be denials. Even if someone in the Czechoslovak government did write that letter, they wouldn't own up to it. They'd be torn apart in the streets."

"Exactly. I came here to use the phone. I tried Dubček's office. No one answered. Then I tried President Svoboda's office. Someone picked up, but they wouldn't tell me anything. Actually, nobody knows where Dubček is. It's strange. So I tried the party official I know."

"That is strange. But this official sounds useful."

Josie wanted to ask the name of the official, but journalists — even when they knew each other well — had to be careful about revealing their sources. She didn't know the name of her own contact, so she couldn't reveal it even if she wanted. But she hadn't told this reporter what she did know, what the Shrouded Man had told her. And she didn't want to. Not yet.

Josie saw from Laurent's expression that he was making his own calculations, deciding what to reveal about his own source, what to keep confidential.

"He's someone I met a few months ago in a bookstore. We struck up a conversation and became friends. He's hard to reach at the moment, like everyone else. How about you? Why aren't you out there reporting on the streets?"

"I have business to take care of first."

"That sounds mysterious. I wonder if it's related to your stranger on the bridge."

Josie thought for a moment. Here she was, sitting in a café with this young man, chatting, while history happened outside. The time passed easily with him. Josie felt a comfort she hadn't experienced since arriving in Prague. He was eager and forthright, more open than he needed to be. Could she confide in him? Could he help?

She had worked hard to prove herself. She had always believed you earned respect on your own. To accept help was to concede defeat. But maybe, now, she could use a companion.

She was about to say more about the Shrouded Man, and the Commander's threat, when Laurent looked at his watch again and got up abruptly.

"I apologize, but my contact is on the move, and I'm trying to catch him. I should get to Prague Castle before he leaves. It's a shame. One of us always seems to be coming when the other is going."

"Like the Beatles song," Josie said.

"What?"

"'Hello, Goodbye.' The song."

"Oh? You must tell me about it the next time we meet. Just promise me ..."

"Yes?"

"That there will be a next time. Be careful."

He dropped coins on the table and rushed out of the Slavia. Josie finished her coffee and called the waiter over.

She added a generous tip to the check and placed it in his palm, pressing on it.

"I need to find the Café Skrýš. Can you tell me where it is?"

THE CASTLE

Prague Castle rose from the top of the hill. If Laurent turned around he could see the river with its bridges, the old town, and the rest of the city, all of it under attack. He knew no place was safe. But he couldn't help the feeling that by continuing straight ahead, he was walking into the lion's mouth.

The path was strewn with signs of the invasion. Gashes in the asphalt. Crumbled curbstones. Smashed trees. Tracks that ripped through the pretty gardens. The Castle would have been the first place the invaders aimed to take. Dubček would have been there, President Svoboda, other leaders. It housed the halls of government. The beating heart of the nation.

Then Laurent saw the tanks themselves.

They parked in lines with their barrels pointed at the gates. Soldiers dotted the outer courtyard. It was ordinarily a bustling compound, but now it resembled a ghost town. There were no protesters here.

Laurent sensed the tension. It hung heavy on the shoulders of the Czechoslovak guards who sat slumped on the ground, unarmed, and on the Soviet soldiers who stood over them.

Laurent wondered if he'd been smart to come here.

He'd already collected all the official reactions he needed. His persistence and legwork had paid off, and he'd known who to call and where to find them. He'd also known which officials spoke English, so he wouldn't need one of the newspaper's translators, in short supply today. Czechoslovakia had long been a closed country, where few people spoke other languages. In recent years more had been learning.

When he'd asked them about the letter in the Eastern Bloc newspapers, they'd all given more or less the same answer: *nonsense*. He'd followed up with other questions. Was the government still functioning? Would the party session planned for tomorrow still take place? Would there be a shakeup in the Central Committee and the Presidium?

All said yes to the first two questions, no to the third. But to Laurent, none seemed certain. They'd been hesitant. Nervous.

No one used the word "coup." They sounded afraid. But that's what it was bound to be, a coup, backed by Soviet military might.

His contact, the party official he'd befriended, would give him more. He had to find him.

Laurent had called Janek Mrož's office twice. The first time, the aide who answered said Mrož had gone to the police station. But by the time Laurent had arrived, Mrož had come and gone. When Laurent called again from the Slavia, the Aide said he'd headed to Prague Castle.

It was under siege, the Aide had said. He could try there if he dared.

Now, directly ahead, blocking the entry gate, stood three armed Soviet soldiers, examining papers. All Laurent had was his press card, his pen and notebook, and his wits. He was suddenly aware how much he was sweating under his shirt.

He took a long, deep breath. He marched forward.

The first soldier didn't hesitate. The moment he saw Laurent he raised his hand, ordering him to halt.

"You can't be here. Go back to your university. You have no business here."

Laurent knew what the soldier meant. Young black men in Prague, and Eastern Europe generally, tended to be students from abroad. They came from African countries allied with the Soviets, to study — or be indoctrinated into — the communist system. Angola, Mozambique, a handful of others — even Ethiopia. The Soviets and other host countries saw them as tools in a global campaign against the West. In return, the Soviets supplied arms to their governments. The United States, France, and their Western allies, of course, also campaigned for allies in Africa, and rewarded them in the same way.

Laurent had seen African students here in Prague treated dismissively, in spite of the communist rhetoric trumpeting equality of the races. He'd heard the belittling remarks spoken behind their backs, or to their faces. He'd been on the receiving end himself, of both the indifference and the hostility. So when he showed the soldier his press pass and received a skeptical eye, he wasn't surprised.

"I'm a French journalist. I write for *Paris Flash.*"

The soldier looked unfazed.

"I'm searching for a friend, a Czech official. Janek Mrož."

This time the soldier raised an eyebrow. The one next to him whispered in his ear, and he waved Laurent through.

The experience made Laurent hopeful to find Mrož. It could mean he was still here, on the castle grounds.

Janek Mrož had been the best source he'd found in Prague, and the only one who treated him with respect. He'd gone beyond that, even.

Laurent recalled the first time he met the politician.

That was how he thought of him. Mrož was more than a party functionary — he was a politician in the best and truest sense: charismatic, inspired, inspiring. In private, Mrož gave you all his attention. He made you believe there was no one else in the world. Yet in public, he could draw a crowd, sway it, and make it swell.

The first time they met, in the bookstore, Laurent had recognized Mrož from pictures, but Mrož had been the one to approach him.

"Is that Rimbaud you're reading?"

It took Laurent by surprise. "Yes, it is."

"An inspired poet, if somewhat undisciplined. Tragic that his life was cut so short. But he was a great traveler for someone so young."

"That's right. He lived for ten years in Ethiopia, my homeland. His poetry and travels were inspirations to me."

"Oh?"

"He left his home to travel the world, armed only with his pen. His preparation was the exercise of his imagination. I thought, why can't I do the same?"

Mrož inquired about Laurent's path from Ethiopia to Paris to Prague. He didn't lift an eyebrow when Laurent said he was a journalist, which was unusual. As a black reporter for a French newspaper, Laurent tended to surprise people when he produced his press card. They tended to underestimate him.

He could use that to his advantage. But it could also be taxing. It made him all the more persistent in his search for answers.

They continued their conversation over coffee at the Café Slavia, exchanging views on favorite books and discussing writers who'd lived in Prague. Laurent expressed his admiration for

Kafka. Mrož confessed that he thought the famous Czech writer was overrated. He admitted he wrote poetry himself.

"It's not very good, but I find it soothing," Mrož had said. "To arrange one's thoughts in patterns that please the ear."

Laurent told Mrož how his own love of literature had grown, starting with the Amharic poetry he'd learned as a child.

"They were like riddles, and my father made games out of them. He crafted poems that would say one thing but hint at its opposite, and we had to figure out the double meaning. It's traditional in Ethiopia. Our poets mask insults with praise, a gentle form of rebellion against the powerful. It's why I've always liked poetry. Every poem has the potential to hold a mystery. If you read it, reread it, speak it out loud, the mystery might reveal itself."

"Your father was a poet. And you follow in his footsteps, because you make your living by words."

"I suppose you're right. I never thought about it like that. But I do I believe that literature helps us make sense of the world. And helps us empathize with people who are different."

"For me, the point of literature is to show us how we can change the world, to compel us to improve it." Mrož had looked wistful for a moment. "If only society could be as beautiful and orderly as a sonnet."

Laurent had recited lines from a poem he knew by heart, a favorite, Lewis Carroll's "Jabberwocky." It was not a sonnet, and it was definitely not orderly. But it was beautiful. Mrož had laughed.

"I suppose we are both idealists of different sorts. As a journalist, your goal is to explain the world. As a public servant, mine is to organize it."

And so they began to debate the purpose of poetry, the power of ideas, and the meanings of literature.

They met from time to time in cafés over coffee, and in beer gardens over pilsners. They talked about books, but Laurent also asked Mrož for background on stories he'd been assigned, and Mrož sought Laurent's views on world events. It was an easy friendship. It suited them both. Mrož was a friend and a source, but also a mentor, someone to help Laurent navigate a new world. Passersby would recognize the politician and stop to chat. They shared their woes and their hopes with him, and he responded with warmth and charm. The people of Prague loved him.

But the last time Laurent had seen him, Mrož had seemed agitated. There'd been rumors of growing tensions in the government.

"If there is a shakeup in the party," Laurent had asked, "who comes out on top?"

The politician had smiled. "The party members are strong-willed and dedicated. They will follow the right course. We will come together for safety and prosperity, and I am confident they will choose a leader with the best interest of the nation at heart, in spite of any crisis."

The answer took Laurent by surprise. It was too glib. It didn't sound like the man he'd come to know. He saw a glint in the politician's eye. It almost sounded like Mrož had been talking about himself.

Well, Laurent had thought, a leader needs a degree of self-confidence.

Now, as he entered the Castle's inner courtyard, he searched for his friend. Soldiers stood in lines at attention next to the fountain in the middle. Two orderlies carried a bleeding, bandaged man out of a building. Laurent saw several men who worked in the administration. They stood in a cluster near the wall, stooped. He could see how they felt the halls of government were no longer their own. It was because they couldn't make out what lay ahead, even a few hours into the future. Laurent saw their fear.

He searched the windows on upper floors of the stately buildings. Some were cracked, shot out by machine guns. None showed any signs of life. Beyond, the spires of St. Vitus Cathedral touched the clouds.

Laurent approached a man he recognized. Where was Mrož? The man had seen him earlier and said Mrož had been able to get into the Castle, past the soldiers blocking entrances. Laurent heard awe in the man's voice. He chalked it up to Mrož's skill with people.

"You'd better leave while you can," the man told Laurent. "We're stuck here. You don't want to be too."

A crack divided the air like sudden thunder. Heavy artillery — but where?

A division of olive-uniformed soldiers entered the courtyard, running in step. Shouts broke out.

"You!" The voice came from behind Laurent. The barrel of a gun pressed against his back. "You don't belong here. Show me your papers."

Laurent raised his arms and turned. A Soviet officer was pointing an assault rifle.

"I'm a French journalist." Laurent reached down, tentatively, to pull out his press pass once again. "Here —"

A stream of Russian came from the gate. The soldier who'd let Laurent through was pointing at the castle opposite. The two Soviets conversed in barks and queries.

Laurent could not leave without finding Mrož. He needed answers. With the officer distracted, he could slip away. A couple of men in suits were entering the Castle not far off, and he could follow them in. He told himself the Soviets wouldn't shoot.

Then the officer spoke. "You're free to go," he said, sweeping his rifle toward the gate. "You must leave immediately. Prague Castle belongs to us now. In any case, the man you seek has gone to party headquarters."

Whatever they'd said to each other, it was a gift. Laurent didn't question it.

Besides, he had no objection to leaving the Castle now. He had to get to the Central Committee Building to find Mrož before he filed his piece. He knew his friend could give him a deeper angle that would make his story stand out.

Outside, Laurent checked his watch. It was too late. His editors were waiting, and his time was up. He had to return to the hotel and give them what he had.

All of Prague's terrain — its ancient streets, but also its social conventions and way of life — were trembling now, like the aftershock of an earthquake. Or tremors that anticipated another. Laurent felt like the worst was yet to come.

Mrož had been his anchor in this city and this job. Laurent needed him now more than ever. But the odds of catching up with him seemed to dwindle by the minute.

The Hotel

Laurent made his way through the crowds, watching the way they mocked their invaders, listening to their chants, observing the types of armored vehicles still moving into the city. He resigned himself to the fact that he wasn't going to see his friend, his source, until later in the day, if at all. Dejected, he pressed on for the hotel.

As he walked, the city fell deeper into chaos.

No longer paralyzed by dismay, the residents of Prague faced off against the endless parade of metal monsters. They built barricades against them out of trucks, bulldozers, furniture, anything they could find. They left Radio Prague — the heart of a populace hungry for information, now denied — and massed in new locations. They cried out in anguish as planes with unfamiliar shapes roared overhead.

The Hotel International, when it appeared, was both imposing and serene. Outside the city center, it appeared to resist the madness. Modeled on the massive towers Stalin had built in Moscow to symbolize Soviet power, the structure reminded those who'd come here from Prague's quainter streets who was ultimately in charge. A red star shimmered atop its peak, higher in the sky than all but a single church steeple in this City of a Hundred Spires.

Tanks squatted on the driveway, but no protesters challenged them here. Soldiers carried long guns with bayonets and wore caps bearing the emblems of Warsaw Pact nations. The Soviets had sent garrisons from Bulgaria, Poland, Hungary … all puppet allies. Their might could not be questioned. But where were the defending troops? Why had an absent military left it to the people to make a stand for Czechoslovakia?

Chaos had managed to seep into the hotel lobby. Tourists and businessmen streamed across the marble, which magnified the drumbeats of pattering feet. Hysteric voices rose over the bustle.

Laurent weaved through the dense, panicked crowd with his hands in his pockets. At the front desk, people queued up to complain about the phones and the electricity. The lines had been cut hours ago. If the invaders wanted to limit communications with the outside world, they'd targeted the right building.

Laurent reflected on his situation. He found himself in the middle of history-making events, but like he'd told Josie, and in spite of the interest she'd showed, he knew he'd been sent on little more than a journalistic errand.

Still, like he told Josie, he did believe he was lucky to be here. He recalled what his editor had said back in Paris, before he'd left for Prague. The words had boosted his pride, but they also issued a warning.

"I'm taking a chance on you, Laurent. You're a brilliant writer. You're driven. There's no one else on the entire staff like you. But you have a lot to learn."

"I understand, sir. I won't let you down."

"I won't mince my words. You have a tendency to veer off the tracks. People are waiting for you to fail. I don't need to go into that, do I? You're aware."

"It's not the first time people have doubted me. I'll play by the rules. I'll make you proud. My university professor too."

It might have been a promise he was bound to break.

An American movie crew filed through the hotel lobby, lugging heavy cases and big metal film cans. Laurent sidled up to a man with a tripod over his shoulder.

"What's going on? I didn't know Hollywood was filming in Prague."

"Not in the city," the man said. "Near Davle, on the outskirts. We're making a World War II picture. Or we were, anyway. We've got tanks and armored trucks and jeeps down there, loaned by the Austrians. But we don't want to get blown up for looking like the enemy. We're organizing convoys out of the country now in whatever ordinary vehicles we can find."

"That makes sense. I heard all the airports are closed."

"Yeah, the roads are the way out of this madhouse. But we're leaving millions of dollars in equipment behind. The producers are having fits. And we have to go real soon. They say the Soviets are going to block the roads tomorrow. And close the borders, maybe sooner."

"Where did you hear that?"

"Our embassy. The American Ambassador ordered us out of the country. Nonessential personnel and all that. I can't say I disagree. Are you leaving too?"

"No, I'm staying. I'm a correspondent for *Paris Flash*."

"I guess that's your job. But if you change your mind, join us. We're taking a few Czechs who need to leave too — we're going to hide them. The last convoy leaves at seven tonight, by the road south to Austria. We're passing Davle to pick up the rest of our crew and any gear we can salvage."

"I hope I won't have to. This is a big story. But it's kind of you to offer."

"If anyone gives you trouble, tell them Freddy sent you."

"Thanks, Freddy. I'm Laurent."

"Good luck to you."

They shook hands, and the man hurried off to catch up with his crew.

Laurent climbed two flights of stairs to the *Paris Flash* bureau. He nodded at the desk clerk and pulled a chair up to a typewriter.

He tried to focus on typing up the quotes he'd collected, but his mind wandered to what Freddy had told him. Did the Soviets really plan to blockade the city? And if they did, what was the point? To stop people coming in, or going out?

Laurent knew one person who would have the answers.

Mrož.

If Laurent could get the details before a blockade began, the bureau chief would be impressed.

Laurent finished his copy and whisked the page out of the typewriter. He dropped it in the tray on the clerk's desk. The clerk would get the story to Paris as soon as the bureau had a line out of the country. It was out of his hands.

The chief would expect Laurent to check in and pick up a new assignment. He would want Laurent to wait here for instructions. No doubt he would give him another piece of busywork.

He thought of his editor's reprimand. It had been a warning. *People are waiting for you to fail.*

Should he stay or go? He remembered how hard it was to get this far in the job. He glanced at the clerk's tray, and out the window. The city awaited.

He dashed out of the office and raced down the stairs. He left the hotel through a back exit. He wanted to avoid the bureau chief so he would be free to pursue the new lead. He could make excuses later. By that time, he would have a new story. A big one.

Laurent walked out into the daylight. Prague seemed full of possibility now, in spite of the new columns of smoke he saw rising over the rooftops. He forgot about minor errands. He felt a courage well up inside, emboldening him to brave the forces overtaking the city.

But instead of thinking about Mrož, he found himself thinking about someone else entirely.

He was thinking about Josie Brouk. About the path she'd started down, and her mysterious stranger on the bridge. And the police. It could only lead to trouble.

He wondered where she was. He wondered if she was safe.

THE ATTACK

Laurent focused on finding Mrož, this time at the Central Committee Building. He wasn't hopeful he'd find him there, or that he'd even make it past the inevitable cordon of Soviet troops. But he had to try.

He managed to hail a taxi. Traffic snarls made the journey slow. A couple of times a view opened between buildings and Laurent saw the Castle rise in the distance, stretched along the long hill above the river. He shivered at the thought of the close call he'd had there.

Traffic got thicker, detoured through narrow lanes by street closings and the columns of military vehicles. The driver became anxious. Soon he told Laurent he could no longer proceed. He apologized and confessed that he planned to flee the city. His family had a house in the country. He seemed to think leaving Prague would allow him to escape the nation's fate.

The driver left Laurent on the curb. Wenceslas Square was close. He'd walked a block when the plaza opened up before him, and he saw why the driver had been so anxious to leave.

The square had become the heart of conflict between troops and protesters.

It was alive with hundreds, *thousands*, of people massed around tanks. They locked arms and marched. They cheered, chanted, moaned. They whistled and jeered and shouted. The tanks seemed to float in a sea of people. Someone raised a flag of brilliant colors — white, red, and blue — into the air, and Laurent watched it ripple in the breeze. The banner brought shouts.

"Go back to Russia!"

"No one wants you here!"

"Nazis!"

The epithet shocked Laurent, but he understood why they'd used it. The Soviets had once cleared out those vicious invaders. Now they'd taken their place.

Machine-gun fire rattled the air. Laurent ducked behind a tram that sat abandoned on its tracks. A cable running overhead snapped and fell to the ground, buzzing and whipping.

At the end of the wide boulevard stood the National Museum. Bullet holes pockmarked the front. Fresh scars ran up and down its pillars. Chunks of stone fell off the statues that decorated its grand facade, limbs and crowns and other body parts. A figure toppled from the roof as Laurent watched, dust following it down like the trail of a spiraling plane.

A man stood nearby at the edge of a crowd, his jaw hanging open.

"You're destroying our treasures," he shouted. "Our pride! Stop shooting!"

The soldiers paid no attention. Another bystander answered him.

"They think it's the Parliament building. Fools!"

Somehow, the statue of the city's patron saint and guardian, St. Wenceslas, sat unscathed atop his horse, high over the crowds and cobblestones in front of the museum. In defiance of the attacking troops, he raised his banner to the sky.

More gunfire ricocheted off buildings like they were canyons. Sirens rang out. Volunteers lifted an injured man onto a stretcher as he treated his own leg wound with a makeshift tourniquet.

All around, young people thrust placards over their heads, championing peace, love, Dubček, freedom. Laurent thought of the civil rights campaigns by black Americans and the student movements sweeping France and the United States. Their spirit had come to Prague.

In those other countries, a backlash had followed the protests. Police responded with brutal violence. Martin Luther King Jr., the American minister and civil rights leader, had been assassinated. Then Robert F. Kennedy, the charismatic young politician running for president, had been shot too. Would the same fate befall Alexander Dubček, or the other Slovak and Czech leaders, who dared to defy the Soviet overlords?

A tank swerved, and screams rose from people in its path. Some fell to the street. Others ran. More rushed in and crowded around the tank. The rising intensity made Laurent nervous. But he focused on the task he'd set himself, to reach the Old Town Square, where the Central Committee Building was located.

Laurent was nearly out of Wenceslas Square and on his way when he saw a group of protesters surrounding a tank that had stopped. They didn't shout or throw objects. They showed no anger at all. They simply spoke to the soldiers riding on top, trying to engage them in conversation. One hung a wreath of flowers over the long gun barrel. Another offered a soldier a cigarette. He ignored her. He could have been younger than the students. A girl approached with a paintbrush in hand. She wrote a single word in Russian on the heavy armament. *Pochemoo.*

Laurent knew what it meant: *Why?*

He had no answer himself. The whole mess seemed absurd. A communist party already ruled the country, and it posed no threat to the military supremacy or fundamental orthodoxy of the Soviets. All the reformers wanted was greater freedom of expression, not even full-fledged capitalism. What did the Soviets plan to do with the country?

The tank with the writing on its side plowed ahead, right through the protesters, whose only aim had been to question violence and advocate peace. That was all they wanted, but it swept them aside.

The tank drew close, and Laurent stood in its path. An angry crowd gathered around. It wasn't a good place to be — if he wanted to find Mrož in one piece, he had to move.

He recalled the painted word. *Why?* He didn't leave the road. Instead, he stepped back so the tank would pass within arm's reach. As soon as it roared close, he matched its pace and called up to the soldier.

"I'm a correspondent for *Paris Flash.*" He tried French, then English. "What are your orders? What is it you're doing here?"

The soldier wore a gray jumpsuit. Soot covered his cheeks. He was nervous and quiet.

"I heard there's a plan to blockade the city. Is it true?"

The soldier leveled his gaze. Laurent kept up.

"What were you told to expect when you got here? I want to know your side. Tell me your story."

That did the trick. The soldier turned to Laurent. His eyes were bloodshot, tired, fearful.

"My crew and I were flown in overnight, and we didn't know where we were. An hour ago I thought I was in Minsk! Then our commanders told us we came to protect. They told us the people would greet us as liberators, like in 1945. Not curse at us or call us Nazis. I don't understand! A blockade? They don't tell us anything. Please, tell *me* what's happening!"

The tank lurched forward and left Laurent in its wake. He watched for a moment as the crowd surged around him, filling the gap it left, then crossed the square to make his way toward the heart of the Old Town.

The soldier's answer disturbed him. How many mere boys had no idea where they were or why they'd been sent? Someone, somewhere, had lined them up, put them in their places, and sent them across the map, like a chess master moving pawns across a vast board in the most dangerous game of all.

Laurent hadn't been walking five minutes when he spied a familiar figure.

Josie Brouk.

She walked with determination, checking each of the storefronts she passed.

She was heading away from Laurent, but he could afford a small detour. He couldn't ignore the coincidence. He was still concerned, and he wanted to speak to her.

He was about to cross the street and hail her when he noticed another figure trailing a block behind — a man in a long coat with one hand in his pocket. He lingered at windows and moved in spurts.

Laurent thought back to the police station. He'd been right. They'd followed her.

He waited for both Josie and the man to move, then followed for several blocks to confirm his suspicion. At one point Laurent thought he might have been spotted. But the man showed no further signs, so he kept going.

Josie turned at the next street. Laurent slowed his pace until the man disappeared around the corner too. He knew he had to be cautious, but he couldn't lose them. So he burst ahead and turned the corner.

He nearly collided with the man in the trench coat, who stood there facing him, tall and grim, with a gun in his hand.

Laurent's first thought was still for Josie. Over the man's shoulder, she was nowhere in sight. The street was narrow and short, almost an alleyway. It contained no shops, only recessed entryways leading to ancient residences. Paint peeled off crumbling walls, and chunks of plaster and cement lay on the pavement. Outlets branched to the left and right, but the street led to a dead end.

If Josie wasn't here, that meant she'd made it to the next street. Laurent might not be able to catch up, but no matter — he'd delayed her stalker. He could help her lose the tail.

But now the danger was his.

Laurent raised both hands.

"Don't shoot. I'm a journalist."

The man opposite him didn't seem to take the words as a warning so much as a confirmation. The small straight line of his mouth edged up at the corners into a tight smile. Laurent stepped backward.

The man raised the barrel of his gun slowly until it pointed forward, eye level with Laurent. Panic seized him. He knew the man was going to kill him, and there was nothing he could do about it. He was going to be dead in seconds.

But no scenes from his life passed before his eyes. Not of home, not of Paris or Addis Ababa or the village he'd grown up in. No memories of his family, or friends, or university, or the places and people he'd met while writing for *Paris Flash*.

He had time for a single image. It was from earlier that day, and it filled his mind. He saw Josie smiling at him, as she'd sat across the table in the Café Slavia.

THE RIDDLE

The gunman's arm tensed, and his eyes popped wide. His mouth made a perfect circle of surprise. He fell forward, face first, knees buckling. He squeezed the trigger as he fell, and a violent report split the air.

Laurent felt a sharp pain in his shoulder.

Behind the gunman stood Josie, holding a brick, like an avenging angel from his imagination. She had one foot on the sidewalk and one in the recessed doorway behind her.

"You're bleeding," Josie said. She stepped forward and took his arm. A red stain marred the sleeve of his linen suit jacket.

Laurent groaned.

Josie wore a green silk scarf at her neck. She pulled it off.

"This was a gift from my grandmother. But she was a practical woman. She would approve."

She tied it above Laurent's bicep and pulled gently on both ends.

"That's kind of you, but—"

"The bullet nicked you. I'm sorry. I should have hit him harder."

"You're sorry? You saved my life!"

"Does it hurt? Do you need a hospital?"

"They have bigger problems. It's not so bad."

Laurent touched the wound. The man who inflicted it was not going to be happy when he woke.

"We should get out of here."

In minutes they were on the next street and around another corner.

Josie checked the makeshift bandage, stained beyond repair. Laurent watched her.

"That man didn't think twice about killing me. When I said I was a journalist, it only made him more eager. What are you mixed up in, Josie Brouk?"

"I don't know. Something serious if police are firing guns."

"That man wasn't regular police. More like StB. State Security."

Laurent let Josie lead the way deeper into the Old Town. The streets, always crooked here, drew sharper angles. He didn't ask her where she was going, and he kept quiet about his own destination, which now fell to the back of his mind. Instead, he watched her examine shop signs and landmarks and peer down the slim alleys Czechs liked to call mouseholes.

The buildings seemed to embrace them as they walked. The cobblestone lanes narrowed and the facades grew taller, like a sheltering canopy, blocking out the rest of the world.

Laurent realized he was lost. The tiny lanes between buildings were becoming more common. They might be in the vicinity of Štupartská Street, but he couldn't be sure.

Josie slowed her pace and sighed.

"Did you follow me all the way from the Slavia?"

"No!"

"You have to admit, it's quite a coincidence, finding me."

"I've been busy. But as soon as I spotted you, I saw him too. I wanted to catch up and warn you, but, well, you know what happened next. Anyway, I told you I was concerned."

"And I told you I could fend for myself, remember?"

"And for me too, apparently."

"I knew he was following me. He's not very good at his job. And I haven't led him to anything yet. I can't find the place I'm looking for."

Laurent studied Josie's features as they walked, how she wrinkled her nose in a certain way. He didn't want to press her. If she wanted to reveal what she was up to, she would. She hadn't said to leave. In fact, he sensed that she wanted him alongside her, and he hoped he was right.

"How about you?" she said. "Did you find your politician friend?"

"Not yet. I'm starting to feel like I'm chasing the White Rabbit."

"You and me both."

"Your man from the bridge?"

"The Shrouded Man. He had a cryptic message for me."

"He sounds more like the Mad Hatter."

"The police chased him. He jumped in the river to escape."

"He jumped!" A dull pain flared from Laurent's wound. "Kafka has a story about a man who jumps in that river. His own father curses him to death by drowning."

"Does the man survive?"

"No."

"Oh."

"There's another story. About St. John of Nepomuk. He's one of the statues on the Charles Bridge. He protects people from drowning and floods."

"I know that one. He took confession from a queen, and the king threw him into the river when he refused to reveal what she'd said."

"Maybe he protected your Shrouded Man."

"I hope so. My Shrouded Man told me to go to a café and mentioned a playwright. The Café Skrýš. Do you know it?"

"Never heard of it."

"I have the address, but addresses aren't helping today."

"What do you mean?"

Josie pointed. A woman was climbing a ladder. She wedged a crowbar behind a street sign and pried it off the wall. A stack of metal plates lay on the ground, some with numbers. Farther down, a couple more students struggled with other plaques. An old woman sat on a bench fanning herself, watching them.

"They appear to be taking apart their own city," Laurent said.

Josie approached the old woman.

"Excuse me. What are they doing to the street signs?"

"Clever young people," the woman answered. A grin crept across her jowled face. "They want to make it difficult for the foreign soldiers. It will become a maze where strangers get lost."

It was clever, Laurent thought. But it would make their search harder.

"One more question, if you don't mind," Josie said. "Do you know where we can find the Café Skrýš?"

"Of course. It's two streets down on the left. There's no sign, but people here know it well enough. You'll recognize it by the blue door."

Josie thanked the old woman and led Laurent down the street.

"He told me not to trust anyone."

"Your Shrouded Man?"

"Yes."

"I'm sure he had good reason."

Josie knew she had to make the decision she'd been able to avoid earlier. They'd be there soon.

"I want to trust you."

"And I want to help. But if you prefer me to leave, I will."

"I have a feeling you wouldn't, even if I asked."

"That might be true."

"I suppose your honesty counts for something."

"I owe you my life. I'll do whatever I can."

Josie made up her mind.

"The Shrouded Man said the strangest thing to me. *I am the walrus.* He told me a playwright would understand. He said freedom hung in the balance, and that it could change the course of history."

"That settles it. He is the Mad Hatter. What does it mean? Does the Prague Zoo have a walrus?"

Josie laughed. Some of the tension lifted.

"No, I think it was a musical reference. To the song by the Beatles, 'I Am the Walrus.' John Lennon sings it."

"That is strange. Especially for someone running from the police."

"It must be a riddle. It contains a message, but I don't know what. So I'm trying to find this café."

"Could it be a code name, the Walrus?"

"That's what I'm thinking."

"Hmm. Then what's the message? What else did he say?"

Josie frowned.

"One word. *Listen.*"

"How well do you know the song?"

"By heart."

"Could the message be in the lyrics?"

Laurent found himself becoming as invested in the Shrouded Man as Josie was, and he suspected she could tell. He was glad she'd opened up.

"It's full of ideas and images that don't seem to make sense," she said. "But it's about attitude. It's rebellious, and poetic. Actually, you mentioned the Mad Hatter. The Walrus comes from *Alice in Wonderland*."

"Oh, I get it now. There's a poem called 'The Walrus and the Carpenter' in *Through the Looking-Glass*. It's a sequel to *Alice*."

Laurent closed his eyes and recalled the lines.

"'The time has come,' the Walrus said,

To talk of many things:

Of shoes — and ships — and sealing-wax —

Of cabbages — and kings —

And why the sea is boiling hot —

And whether pigs have wings.'"

"That makes about as much sense as the song," Josie said. "No wonder John Lennon is a fan."

"Lewis Carroll used absurdity to make people laugh. But he also used it to make a point. The nonsense from his stories is surprisingly logical. He was a mathematician by training. Although his fans go overboard trying to find symbolism. Like Kafka, another absurdist. People can't resist scouring his work for meanings that may not be there."

"People do the same with Beatles lyrics. They hang on every word."

"They're in good company! In the Carroll poem, the Walrus is walking along the beach with the Carpenter, and the Walrus invites a group of Oysters to join their stroll. They line up in droves. The Walrus seems pleasant but in truth he wants to eat them. He expresses regret about tricking the poor oysters, but it doesn't stop him from feasting."

"He sounds horrible."

"He is. Alice doesn't get it at first — she thinks he's being nice, like the Oysters do. She's confused by a lot of what she sees and hears in the book, understandably."

"I wonder if John knew he was singing about a villain. He loves the Alice stories. He uses them in other songs too. 'Lucy in the Sky with Diamonds' takes place in a setting a lot like Wonderland. He wouldn't want to be seen as a monster."

Josie stopped.

"Oh my god."

"What?"

"The Shrouded Man said *I am the walrus*. He said *Listen*. If you're right, and he meant not listen to him, but to the song's lyrics, it changes everything."

"What do you mean?"

"Don't you see? Maybe the Shrouded Man knows the poem. Maybe what he tried to tell me, what he wants the Playwright to know, is a warning. About another monster."

The Hideout

There was no sign of the café. And when Josie and Laurent doubled back, they nearly missed the narrow passage leading off the street for a second time.

They found the Skrýš tucked inside that crevice. It was a small establishment with a lavender awning and a single long window. Though it wasn't well lit within, they could see customers at the tables.

"This is it," Laurent said. "The blue door."

Splinters stuck out of the thick paint like fur on a frightened animal.

At the Slavia, Laurent remembered, no one had noticed or cared when he'd made his phone calls or talked with Josie. It had been big, and crowded. When they entered the Skrýš, heads turned. The patrons of this smaller café took note of newcomers. They cast sly looks, then resumed conversations.

A waiter, a teenager, came and showed them to a table. He took their order, two coffees. As he was about to walk away, Josie stopped him. She motioned, and he leaned down.

"I'm looking for someone who's supposed to be here. A Playwright. I have a message to deliver."

He froze, then hurried away. Josie took it as a good sign. She would wait and see.

Most of the patrons of Café Skrýš were young, another contrast with the Slavia, where intellectuals of an older generation reigned. Here they were largely students, on breaks from protests. Maybe plotting.

Laurent picked up words here and there with the little Czech he knew. Young men with budding goatees and young women with stylish eyeglasses argued about the invaders. Were the soldiers devils, or were they just following orders, and did they deserve sympathy? A copy of Kafka's *The Trial* sat on one table amid demitasse cups and sweet rolls. Laurent leaned in, wondering if the students understood the book's implicit warning.

"They're both Czechs and Slovaks," Josie said. "They're talking about standing together, hand in hand. They refuse to let the Soviets divide them. But they're worried about losing all the freedoms they've gained, to travel, to publish, to read what they want. Since the Prague Spring they've listened to all kinds of music. Now they're scared the records will stop spinning. They're saying they can't let the music die."

Laurent felt like he had talked too much at the Slavia. He enjoyed listening to Josie, and wanted to think about nothing else. Not the clatter of the dishes, the chatter of the students, the threat of violence that hung in the air, or the dangers that lay around every corner, not the secrets that hid behind tight-lipped smiles or the locked doors they had yet to open.

A record player sat on a speaker in the corner, blaring folk music. The song ended, giving way to piano keys, a plaintive voice, and the note of a flute.

"It's the Beatles," Josie said. "'The Fool on the Hill.'"

"Their music seems to follow you around."

It was true, he thought. For the moment, at least, the music couldn't be stopped, not by walls or tanks. The songs found the cracks and pores and wafted through them.

"I love the Beatles," Josie said. "They tell stories and take you places. They make you feel different. Free. Like you could be someone, anyone, whoever you want."

He laughed. "You're passionate."

"People here feel the same. Music sets them free."

"I'm going to listen to the Beatles more! I just remembered — you promised to tell me about a particular song."

"'Hello, Goodbye?'"

"That's the one."

The waiter returned and set down two mugs on saucers and a bowl containing fresh strawberries.

Josie plucked a fruit from the bowl and held it up. "Didn't the strawberry season end?"

"Yes ma'am."

"Where do these come from?"

"The manager knows a farm in Jahodová Pole, south of here. The strawberries are still growing there. It's a miracle."

The information seemed to distract Josie. She tasted a berry. Laurent sipped his coffee.

"My babička would tell me about the strawberry farms outside Prague, where she played as a child. Rows and rows of tiny bushes as far as the eye could see. There was one farmer who let her run wild and pluck the fruits to her heart's delight. The way she described them, I could taste the juice in my mouth. It was her best memory. I remember her whenever I eat them, even more as the summer fades. It brings me closer to her."

Laurent picked up a strawberry too and took a bite. "Have you been there?"

"Sadly, I don't know where it is. She never told me the name of the town, and when she died she took it with her. I haven't been outside the city much, but even if I had the time to explore, I don't know how I'd find it."

"Maybe you'd know it once you saw it. From her descriptions. They sound vivid."

"Maybe. They were."

"My father told me stories about his childhood in the hills in Ethiopia. Now those stories seem more real than my memories. Although I don't think of it as home anymore. The whole place feels distant, like a dream."

From time to time, someone burst into the café and disappeared through the swinging door into the kitchen. They reemerged with the same urgency. Laurent saw Josie watching them too.

Something was going on back there. More than the preparation of coffee and pastries and strawberries.

"The waiter didn't take me seriously," Josie said. She stood up. "I'm going to ask someone else."

She walked to the back of the café. A burly man with a thick mustache and a clean apron stood outside the kitchen, hands on his hips. The manager, no doubt.

"I have a message for the Playwright. It's urgent. I was told to come here."

The manager shrugged and smiled, making a dimple in his cheek.

"Please return to your table, miss. We are very busy."

"You don't understand. I need to speak to him."

"You need to speak to *him?*"

This time, a laugh rose from his belly. Josie went red.

"Now, listen —"

"Miss, you should finish your coffee and be on your way."

"A man risked his life to send me here. He ran from the police and jumped off a bridge. He could be dead now. I will not be on my way."

The manager stiffened and became serious. The commotion was drawing attention. People stared at Josie. Laurent, who'd caught most of their conversation from the table, began to worry she was making a mistake.

"Wait here," the manager said.

He turned abruptly and went into the kitchen.

Laurent raised an eyebrow. Josie motioned him to join her.

After a few minutes, the manager returned.

"Follow me," he said.

They entered the kitchen, made their way past a couple of café workers, and stopped at a door in the back. The manager knocked, whispered, and pushed through.

He led them into a stairwell, past a younger man wearing a muscle shirt. The creaky stairs complained with every step. The landing was dark. He knocked again, told them to wait, and turned to go back down.

The door opened, and two sets of arms pulled them inside.

SIDE TWO

THE PLAYWRIGHT

Josie and Laurent found themselves in a dimly lit room with a wide table against the far wall, stacked with radio equipment.

Laurent's shoulder smarted from his wound, and the tight grip on his arm didn't help. He wriggled and glared. The man holding him let go and walked over to the radio. He sat down and began operating the dials and switches. The man holding Josie went to a window and peeked through drawn curtains, absorbed in whatever was happening below.

A woman in her early thirties occupied a chair pulled back from a café table, which had a mess of papers on it. She crossed her arms.

"Who are you? What is this about a man on a bridge?"

Josie stepped forward.

"I'm a reporter for the *Toronto Post*. I met a Shrouded Man on the Charles Bridge this morning, and he told me to find you. To deliver a message."

"A Shrouded Man? It sounds like you had a nightmare."

"Are you the Playwright?"

"I am a playwright."

"Then the message is for you."

"I don't have time to entertain the fever dreams of foreigners."

"My name is Josie Brouková. My grandparents came from a village outside Prague, between the wars. I may not have been born here, but my babička made sure I felt like I was. Her stories live in me, and so does her country. I come to you on her behalf as much as my own."

The Playwright studied Josie and appeared to make up her mind. She turned her attention to Laurent.

"You don't have grandparents from here. What's your excuse?"

"I'm with her," Laurent said. Josie's speech had both stunned and impressed him. "But I write for *Paris Flash*. I know who you are. Who in Prague doesn't? Your essays and plays, your voice as a leader of the Prague Spring."

A knock came. The Playwright put her ear to the door, unlocked it, and spoke with a young man who appeared in the gap. She handed him a folded paper. He absorbed its contents, gave it back, and left.

It dawned on Laurent what this place was. He'd heard the radio reports. He knew Soviet troops had shut down Radio Prague. The broadcasts continued anyway. They were operating from secret locations.

"You're broadcasting here for Radio Prague."

"Radio Prague is no more. We are Radio Czechoslovakia now. Radio *Free* Czechoslovakia."

Laurent saw the map on the café table, barely concealed under a couple of spiral notebooks. He suddenly understood the importance — and the danger — of what was happening here.

"You're not only broadcasting. You're coordinating other stations too."

"We cannot let the Soviet commissars and their giant metal rats steal our nation, not without a fight. Clandestine radio stations are springing up all over the country. Slovaks, Czechs, Romanis, all together now, as one. In stables, attics, kitchens, farmhouses. Places where hope springs like a miracle. We switch locations and frequencies so the Soviets cannot track us."

"Impressive," Laurent said.

"You're forming a resistance," Josie said.

The Playwright smiled. She could hide her operations from the enemy, but she couldn't conceal her pride from reporters.

The woman motioned them to sit in the chairs opposite her. "We have very few minutes before we go on the air. What is this message?"

"The Shrouded Man said freedom hung in the balance, for everyone." Josie concentrated, trying to remember the exact words. To get them right. "First, he said, *I am the walrus*. Like the Beatles song. Then he told me to go to Café Skrýš. And he said, *Listen. The Playwright will understand.*"

The Playwright waited. Josie fidgeted.

"That is all?"

"There was no more time. The police came. He jumped off the bridge into the river. I don't know what happened to him."

"Let us hope he was a good swimmer. Did he tell you his name?"

"No."

"It sounds like nonsense. But I know this song. Enough to know what it represents, and to know that someone with the Soviets would not mention it. Still, I do not know you. I do not know this Shrouded Man. Like I said, time is—"

Laurent set his jaw and mustered all the confidence he could.

"Look, we didn't have to come here. It's a big risk. If there's a message in the song for you, like we believe, don't you want to know what it is? The man on the bridge knew where he was sending Josie. His message must be important. Can you afford not to know it?"

The Playwright dipped her head, like she knew she was going against her better judgment.

"Perhaps this man is someone I know, or who knows me."

"I think he does," Josie said. "He sounded emphatic that I find you. I know people. I know he was being sincere. He wasn't lying to me."

"Your Shrouded Man said to listen. Let us do that." She motioned to the man at the window. He rushed from the room. "Our staff are young, and they have record collections. Somebody will find the song quickly."

"They won't need to leave the café," Josie said. "The record we need was just playing."

Barely a minute passed before footfalls bounded up the stairs. The man burst in lugging a boxy, lidded turntable in his arms, the one they'd seen in the café below. A record sleeve slid across the top.

The album cover was different from the one Josie owned. It lacked the bright yellow border and was mostly purple. The dimensions were smaller. But it sported the same psychedelic lettering, and the same strange photo in the middle: John, Paul, George, and Ringo wearing cartoonish animal costumes.

It was unmistakable. It was *Magical Mystery Tour.*

Josie knew the U.K. versions of Beatles albums were issued by a different label, Parlophone, than the LP she'd bought in Toronto. Over there, they'd released it as a double EP — two seven-inch discs played at 45 RPM, with a song or two on each side — the first of its kind in Britain.

It contained six songs, all from the soundtrack of the *Magical Mystery Tour* movie the Beatles had made last year. They were "Magical Mystery Tour," "Your Mother Should Know," "I Am the Walrus," "The Fool on the Hill," "Flying," and "Blue Jay Way."

Across the Atlantic, Capitol Records had repackaged the album for Canada and the U.S. They didn't think a double EP would sell in North America, so they changed the album into a standard twelve-inch LP. And they added five more songs, all recent singles: "Hello, Goodbye," "Strawberry Fields Forever," "Penny Lane," "Baby, You're a Rich Man," and "All You Need Is Love."

The man set the turntable down, plugged it in, and opened the lid. He lifted the needle and dropped it onto the groove. The record began to play.

Josie had described the song to Laurent, but she knew nothing could prepare him for the experience. The drama, the chaos, the mania, the quality that sounded almost sinister, the way it mesmerized anyone who heard it.

She watched him strain to hear the words. To understand them.

The song was nearly over. John Lennon sang the final chorus. Backing singers struck up a rhythmic chanting in words that were barely discernible. The chanting gave way to a nightmarish combination of random sounds and orchestral music. The Playwright clenched her teeth.

"You are wasting our time. The song is nonsense. I can make out no message."

"But he said you would understand —"

Bitterness crossed the Playwright's face, like scars on a battle map.

"We have an important announcement to broadcast. Thousands of people are waiting to hear from us. Now get out."

THE MESSAGE

Josie opened her mouth to protest. She wanted to tell the Playwright that the song was full of meaning, real and imagined. She wanted to list all the references the song contained, to actual people and events, to literature, to music. Somewhere in the music or the lyrics, there had to be a clue. She knew it.

The Playwright went rigid. She jabbed her open palm at Josie. "Quiet!"

The Playwright tilted her head. She concentrated.

"Go back fifteen seconds. Turn it up."

The man at the turntable moved to lift the needle but bumped it instead. It ripped across the surface, screeching. He placed it back onto a groove and adjusted the volume knob.

John Lennon's final stanza gave way once again to a long fade-out. Orchestral strings stabbed in rhythm, ascending an infinite scale. Overlapping voices emerged behind them, chanting words that Josie could never make out: *oompah oompah ...* something. They sounded like militarized robots, an invading chorus from another world, absurd and surreal.

Out of the chaos, faint male voices were reciting lines from a play. Josie knew about this part. The Beatles had captured the audio from a BBC broadcast during the recording session. John had wanted to include a random snippet of sound from the radio. Ringo found one. It sounded good to them.

"Switch it off," the Playwright said.

This time her compatriot raised the needle more carefully.

"Start the broadcast," she told the men. To Josie and Laurent, she said, "You two, come with me. Bring the turntable."

Josie picked up the record sleeve, and Laurent unplugged the player. As they followed the Playwright out, they heard the others begin the announcement.

"This is Radio Free Prague. We are broadcasting on three medium wavelengths: 233 meters, 428 meters, 492 meters. Also long wave at 1103 meters. We have important instructions for resisting the invaders ..."

They continued up the stairs and found another room, smaller than the first. The Playwright pointed to a table and a power outlet.

"I know why your Shrouded Man told you to find me. He knew I'd recognize those lines and understand their meaning. He must have known you too, in a sense. He knew the Beatles held meaning for you. Enough to make you curious, to stir you to action."

It explained the Shrouded Man's first remark to Josie. *You are young.* And why he'd said afterward that freedom hung in the balance. *For all of us, young and old alike.*

Laurent thought about the words spoken faintly beneath the music. He knew them from somewhere. A villain, letters, death. Gloucester.

"*King Lear.*" He and the Playwright said it together.

The Playwright lifted the needle arm. She touched it down near the end of the song. The lines played again. Dour voices speaking with dire import. The Playwright joined in and spoke over them, making them loud and clear:

"Slave, thou hast slain me. Villain, take my purse:

If ever thou wilt thrive, bury my body,
And give the letters which thou find'st about me
To Edmund Earl of Gloucester; seek him out
Upon the English party. O untimely death!"
She stopped the record.

"There was more, but that was enough. Do you know the story?"

Josie knew *King Lear* was one of Shakespeare's most famous plays, but she had never read it or seen it performed. *I will now*, she told herself.

"King Lear has three daughters," Laurent said. "He's getting old and decides to give up the throne. But he makes the disastrous decision to split the kingdom up and give it to the two who least deserve it, instead of the one who's loyal and honest. The kingdom falls apart. Lear himself goes mad. It ends in tragedy for nearly everyone. But these lines, I don't remember who speaks them."

"They belong to Oswald, the steward to Lear's scheming daughter Goneril," the Playwright said. "Oswald carries a letter from Goneril to her lover Edmund that plots the death of her husband and total capture of the kingdom."

The Playwright paced, deep in thought, hands behind her back. Josie and Laurent waited.

"This is the message your Shrouded Man wanted me to hear. The meaning is clear. We face more than an invasion — we have an internal enemy as well. That is what King Lear is all about."

To Josie, the room seemed to darken. "That means —"

"Traitors."

"I think it's more specific," Laurent said. "The lines talk about a letter. I've been reporting on a letter that was published this morning in newspapers across the Eastern Bloc. The Soviets say it was written by Czechoslovaks, inviting them to invade. But no one I talked to here believes it."

"The Shrouded Man is telling us the letter is real," Josie said. "Isn't he?"

"This is huge," Laurent said.

They felt the tremors in each other's voices. A story like this — it was the kind they had both dreamed to tell.

The Playwright said, "But the analogy goes further."

"Do you you mean Dubček has gone mad?" Josie asked. "Like King Lear?"

"No, Dubček is not Lear. That role goes to Brezhnev, the old man who made the Soviets' decision to invade. Dubček is more like Lear's honest daughter, Cordelia. And near the end of the play, she is captured by the enemy."

"And Dubček has disappeared," Laurent said.

"Exactly. Early this morning, he appealed to the people in a short radio address. He asked us to forego violence. Since then, no one has heard from him."

"They've taken him."

"It seems likely. But no one knows. I worry the people might believe he betrayed us. Or that his refusal to mount an armed response means we should give up."

Josie had wondered about that. "What did happen to the army?"

"They were ordered to stand down. We don't know why, or who issued the order. I suspect it was the memory of Budapest, still fresh for people. When the Soviets invaded there in 1956, many Hungarian troops took their side, and there was much bloodshed. Our government might have feared a repeat of those events. But there are other ways to resist. The invaders can kill people and destroy monuments. But they cannot shoot ideas."

"You don't have to worry about the spirit of the people," Laurent said. "They're fighting back every way they can."

"For now. But what will the streets look like in a week, or a month? The troops will leave. The Soviets will use even greater weapons, to break our spirit. Not tanks but lies. Lies spread like sickness. They breed fear. They break nations. The Soviets will tell us lies about Dubček, about ourselves, and they will wreak a psychic toll, like they do in their own country already. They will try to divide us, and say that Dubček, a Slovak, has betrayed the Czechs. They will tell us the only solution is to fall in line. I have already seen people holding signs that say *Death to traitors*." The Playwright gestured at the radio equipment. "The people need us. To advocate decency. To fight the lies."

"But if there's a traitor —"

"We need to know who it is," the Playwright said. "We need to tell the people it is not Dubček! To fight the lies, we have to disentangle the truth. But if the song tells the traitor's identity, I cannot discern it. Maybe your Shrouded Man knows. Can you find him again?"

"I don't know anything about him."

"That is unfortunate." The Playwright went to the window and pulled the curtain back an inch. "We ourselves don't have the time to investigate. We're drawn thin as it is."

"We can do it," Josie said. "We can dig around."

"In the middle of an invasion? Your Shrouded Man was scared. Others will be too. They won't know who to trust. Who will talk to you?"

"Leave that to us," Laurent said.

"Your newspapers will think you are chasing a fantasy."

"We'll do it anyway," Josie said.

"Don't tell them. They cannot know, not yet. If the Western press prints the story that Czechs or Slovaks invited the Soviets to invade, our resistance will implode. Rumors of collaborators would send people into a frenzy, set them at each other's throats. That serves only the invaders. Like Lear's kingdom, we'd collapse from the inside."

Josie and Laurent knew they had a decision to make. They knew they had to be of one mind. They could break a story that would win them accolades and respect, the prizes they'd worked for. Or they could keep it a secret, for now — and help the Playwright and her budding resistance find the truth.

Josie took Laurent's hand.

"We won't tell them," he said.

She nodded.

They both knew that the essence of the clandestine network's mission was the same as their own: They found the hidden stories, and they spoke for those who could not be heard. They gave truth a voice.

The Playwright slammed her fist on the table, startling them.

"Today we woke to a city under threat. Tomorrow, who knows? Will we wake as cockroaches, aliens in our own homes? Will we find ourselves dragged into courts with no knowledge of the charges? Will our nation disappear from the map? These things once sounded like tales from Kafka. Today they sound real."

"There's still hope," Josie said. "You just have to know who you can trust."

"You're right, I know you are. Do what you can. Identify the traitor. Find out what happened to Dubček. Then come back and tell us so we can inform our country."

A clatter came from downstairs. A door crashed open. Then heavy footfalls. Furniture thrown. Wood cracking.

And shouts.

In Russian.

THE ESCAPE

Josie still had Laurent's hand in her own. She gripped it tightly. He stepped between her and the door. The Playwright remained calm.

"Take the window. Climb around the ledge to the roof. It will hide you from the street, but stay back as you cross the roofs, and take the first way down you see."

"What about you and your men?"

"They will be hiding the equipment. Go!"

The commotion downstairs had quieted, and no sound came from the stairwell. It was only a matter of time. The Soviet soldiers tearing the café apart would find their way up soon.

Laurent managed to get the window frame up half a foot before it stopped, jammed in place. He and Josie got under it, and together they pushed. It moved and gave them a big enough opening to fit through. Below the window, two soldiers cradled machine guns, both focused on the entrance. They weren't the clueless young men riding on tanks. They were older, hardened. These soldiers knew where they were, and they knew why. Laurent climbed through. Josie followed.

Backs against the building's pastel facade, they sidestepped across the ledge. It ended in a low decorative wall. Laurent stepped over it and extended an arm. Josie gripped the rail and pulled herself across. On the other side, she took his hand again.

They stepped, slid, and jumped over a treacherous terrain of sloping roofs. More than once, they lost their footing. The first set of dormers they came to had locked windows. The second had one ajar, and they slipped into it. A bedroom with a kitchenette, empty. In spite of whatever waited on the other side, they burst through the door, down a hall, to the top of a stairwell. They raced down the steps and found themselves on the street once again.

"Slow down," Laurent said. "We don't want attention."

"I can't believe they found them. Did we lead them there?"

"Who knows. They must be searching lots of places, and getting tips too. I think they had agents in Prague scouting the city before today. The Skrýš could have been a target already."

Laurent recalled the Russian tourists who'd started appearing in Prague in large numbers in recent weeks. No women or children. All men, with short haircuts and military builds, like soldiers on vacation.

They passed a hat shop with an open door. A radio blared. A voice spoke in urgent tones.

"We are sorry to report that our secondary station in Prague has been raided. We are now broadcasting from another location. Tell everyone you know to tune in at this new frequency ..."

The shop manager and two customers listened, unaware that the drama holding them riveted had unfolded just down the street.

Josie was devastated. "Now what?"

"I don't know. But we can't go back there."

"We'll find another way."

Laurent knew she believed it. He wasn't so certain.

"Can you remember any other details about the Shrouded Man? Like the quality of his clothes. Or his shoes. Was his voice distinctive?"

The only part of him Josie could see now were his eyes. They had pierced the dawn, gray but bright. Bold, but scared.

"I've been trying all day to remember more. It was dark, and such a shock, and over so soon."

"Sometimes a memory comes back when you stop trying. Think about something else."

Josie thought for a moment. "How did you become a reporter?"

It caught him off guard, the personal question. But it pleased him to be asked.

"In my village, growing up, I always wanted to know what was happening over the next hill. Nobody would tell me. They wanted to spare me from the troubles that lay beyond.

"Then I heard about a school in Addis Ababa. It was French, so I'd have to learn the language, but I thought I could find the answers I wanted. So I went to the city. I read books. I loved school, but the teachers saw me as a project more than a person. They wanted to shape me to fit their expectations. I had too many questions they couldn't answer, or wouldn't. I had to leave.

"My family never understood. But I no longer belonged in my own home. There was fighting, disease, and hunger in the land. I wanted to understand why, and the answers seemed to lay elsewhere.

"That took me to Paris, to university. I supported myself by proofreading ads for the newspaper. When I discovered they paid people to ask questions for a living, I convinced someone to hire me in the news department. It suits me, asking questions. It helps me escape the labels and roles other people assign me."

"Yet now you take assignments from editors, and answer their questions instead of your own."

He laughed. "I see the irony. But it's a start. And sometimes it's hard to know which questions are most important. How did you come to pursue journalism?"

"At first, it was an excuse to leave college. But it ran deeper than that. I wanted to leave home too, and I knew the newspaper would help me do that. I suppose I had a wanderlust, from hearing my babička's stories. They made me ache to see the places she talked about. And other places, ones you heard about, imagined, that you had to see in person because you knew they'd be wildly different from your imagination. It's silly, but I resented my parents for their journey across the continents, their coming to Canada. They wanted me to settle for a single home, and never leave."

"I'm sure they wanted you to stay there out of love, not to trap you."

"That's true. And I know their journey was traumatic. But I wanted to travel. I couldn't stay."

"I'm glad you didn't."

"Did your parents call you Laurent?"

Laurent laughed again. "No, they named me Melak. It means 'angel' in Amharic. I looked like a cherub, I suppose. I chose Laurent for myself, in Paris. And Josie is a nickname?"

"Yes, for Josefina."

"A proper Czech name."

She had an idea.

"You're going to see your friend, the official ... Maybe he can help us, if I describe the Shrouded Man, tell him as much as I can."

"It's a good idea. He knows everyone. By now he'll be back at the Central Committee Building."

"In the Old Town Square, isn't it? That's not far. Do you trust him?"

"I think so."

"You have to be certain. You heard the Playwright. If he mentions this to anyone, the consequences —"

"We don't have to tell him why."

"Will it be enough to say it's important? In the middle of the invasion?"

"He's my friend. That's enough."

"It seems like anything we try could go wrong."

"Your source knew that too. He came to you anyway. He knows this is bigger than him. It's bigger than us. It's important for the people here. They have to know who they can trust."

"If you trust your contact, I do too."

Laurent pushed aside the doubt that had nagged him earlier, about the way Mrož had sounded. Now he wished he'd asked the Playwright about him. But Mrož had seemed on edge even before that incident. As someone who had ties to both reformers and hard-liners, he'd been under a great deal of pressure. Laurent told himself he'd misinterpreted his friend's tone.

In fact, he suddenly realized that Mrož himself could be Josie's Shrouded Man. Maybe his White Rabbit and her Mad Hatter were one and the same!

But if that were true, why would Mrož go to another reporter instead of him? Had they been under surveillance? If Laurent were to report the story, would it be too obvious who the source had been?

Dispel one doubt, and another rose in its place. But Laurent pushed it aside. Instead, he focused on something else. Incredibly, his and Josie's stories had merged. Now they shared the same mission.

THE SHROUDED MAN

The afternoon sun battled its own invisible demons in the sky, and its rays seemed to fade along their journey. No matter. Today the heat radiated from the ground up.

The most important government buildings were surrounded by tanks, sealing the people off from their leaders. In their absence, the people of Prague rose up anyway. They filled the streets and surrounded the tanks. The air was thick with the heady spirit of protest.

As they walked, Josie and Laurent caught snatches of conversation, and they asked questions where they could. Dubček was still missing. But people began to repeat information and echo rumors. When they realized details were scarce on the streets, they pressed on.

The Old Town Square took them by surprise when it opened up at the end of a narrow lane.

Armored trucks had parked at the ends of the major streets entering the square. More vehicles were approaching. The Old Town's history and monuments had always made it the core of activity in Prague, and the Soviets knew that. But today the square hadn't filled up with protesters like in other spots. The people of Prague had found new symbolic centers for their efforts, perhaps better ones, in Radio Prague and Wenceslas Square.

The open sky, more visible now than from the small streets, was clear and beautiful in spite of the terror, broken only by thin columns of smoke.

But the pavement was rife with holes and trenches, ruined by the heavy treads of the Soviet tanks. The tanks themselves lay ahead, arranged outside a makeshift barricade of machinery and buses and junk, the kind that protesters had erected at Radio Prague and other places. Mounted guns with barrels that were three meters long faced the building behind the barricade, pivoted toward the windows.

Laurent spotted Mrož through a low point in the barricade, standing outside the offices of the Central Committee of the Communist Party of Czechoslovakia. Excited, he waved. Mrož saw him and returned the greeting. He advanced toward Laurent and Josie, past the tanks like they were mere decorations.

Laurent pointed him out to Josie. He had a revolver on his hip. It was old, like it had seen action the first time Soviets rolled into Prague, that time to save the city.

Josie studied him. He was the picture of confidence, the way he had waltzed past the Soviet soldiers. *If this man is the future of Czechoslovakia, it's a bright one*, she thought. Soviets or no Soviets.

Laurent saw the hope on her face, and it heartened him. He knew Mrož had that effect on people.

They advanced, and the man motioned for them to walk around the end of the line of tanks and come through the barricade there.

"Janek, I've been looking for you all day."

"And what a day it has been, my friend. But now you have found me."

"Is it safe in there?"

"Don't worry. Just stay close."

The soldiers seemed to be minding their own business. One lit a cigarette and leaned against his armored vehicle. Another sat cross-legged on top, reclining against the turret and gazing at the sky.

The scene was too quiet. It bothered Josie. Once inside, would they be able to come out? Laurent slowed his pace, and Josie bumped into him.

The soldiers snapped into action. The smoker tossed his stub into the landscaped garden beside the tank. A rumble started inside the metal shells.

Laurent's friend entered the building. Laurent followed him. Josie had an urge to reach for his hand, as she had before. Instead, she dug into her shoulder bag for her notepad and pen. She didn't pull them out but gripped them in her fist. The Soviet troops, she knew, were getting ready to break the barricade.

She passed through the double doors.

In the lobby, Laurent introduced Josie to his friend, calling him Janek. The man seemed to show a glimmer of recognition at her name, which gave Josie a surge of pride. If he knew who she was, that meant she'd made more of a name for herself here than she'd thought. She was sure she'd seen him before, in person or in photos, but she couldn't remember his surname, and Laurent hadn't said it.

His office had few furnishings, but each piece was steeped in the country's history. A timepiece modeled after the clock outside in the square. A couple of black-and-white photos of dignitaries in a vintage automobile. An antique carpet, which was a rare sight. Two desks. Behind the smaller one, a middle-aged man got to his feet as they entered. His hair was slicked back like it was wet. He came forward and said he was the honorable party member's aide. He breathed heavily, like he had asthma. He shook Laurent's hand and turned to Josie.

Immediately the man dropped the binder he was carrying. He fell to his knees to collect it and apologized, stuttering. When he stood back up, he was trembling.

"Don't be an idiot," Janek said. "Do you have the speech?"

"Yes, it's right here." He gave Janek the binder and turned away from Josie.

She'd met this man before. Had she interviewed him once? Or seen him at the National Assembly? His eyes were so intense.

His eyes!

They were all she'd seen before, on a face shrouded by the folds of a scarf, in the half-light of dawn amid a creeping mist.

At first she felt only surprise. Then a joy surged through her. She'd found him. He was alive. Not dead. Not arrested. And he was safe, with someone they could trust. She broke out in a grin. She couldn't contain herself.

"It's you. From the —"

The Aide, unshrouded, did not return her excitement. Instead, he raised his hand to stop the next word.

"— bridge."

It was too late. The Aide looked over his shoulder at his boss, then back at Josie.

A variety of expressions paraded across Janek's face. Surprise. Recognition. Triumph.

It took Josie a split second to decipher what was going on. To connect the dots. The Shrouded Man's message. The Playwright's solution. The dire warning that was part Beatles, part *King Lear*, part *Through the Looking Glass*. The traitors who had sent a letter to the Soviets, inviting them to invade, then arranging for Dubček to disappear.

Laurent's friend pulled the pistol from his holster.

The Aide dove for the exit.

A shot rang out and the Aide fell in mid-flight, halfway to safety, a bullet in the back of his head.

THE METAMORPHOSIS

Janek raised his revolver and swung it casually toward Josie.

She couldn't have moved if she wanted to. Her blood stopped like ice in her veins. Her muscles felt heavy with the weight of the mistake they'd made, coming here. The mistake *she'd* made, saying what she'd said out loud. It caught her off guard. She'd been so thrilled, so relieved, to find him here.

For the first time, she noticed the placard on the larger desk. *Janek Mrož.*

"You're the traitor."

Mrož watched them intently. Laurent looked at him, then at Josie.

"What?"

"Don't you see? The letter to Moscow. The message in the song. The Walrus. The traitor from King Lear. It's him. He did it."

"No. That's impossible."

"Laurent, his name, the word 'mrož' — in Czech, it means 'walrus.'"

Laurent resisted. It couldn't be true that his friend had done what he'd just witnessed. Or that he could be the traitor. There had to be an explanation. A reason why.

"That's wrong. It has to be. Janek, tell her."

Mrož laughed. He gestured with the gun.

"She's clever, Laurent. And mostly accurate. I was not the only one to sign the letter. But it was my idea, and yes, I sent it. Then I heard someone in Prague was contacting foreign reporters about a so-called conspiracy. I wasn't certain the rumors were about me, but I had to be sure. So I put tails on correspondents. None took the bait — until you. I never imagined the source was my loyal aide. I suppose I should have considered it. I did send communiqués to the Soviet Ambassador from this very office. He must have seen me. I admit, he was more intelligent than I gave him credit for. He liked the Beatles, you know, and that song. Do you see the irony? Today, I am the walrus. Tomorrow, with the help of the Soviets, I'll be the leader of Czechoslovakia."

He spoke without a trace of self-consciousness.

"All you are is a coward," Josie said. "The man you shot, the one who risked his life on the bridge, he's the hero."

"No." Laurent struggled to form words. A wave of nausea fell over him as the truth dawned. "I can't bear this, Janek. What have you done?"

Josie felt a rush of emotion on the verge of pouring out. It felt raw and unspecified, and it rose from anger, over the life of the man who'd trusted her, the man whose secret she had exposed. She couldn't tell whether she was angrier at the traitor standing before her or at herself. Grief and shame rolled over one another in the bottom of her gut.

"You betrayed your country." The words came without direction or will. "Your own people! And your friend."

Next to her, Laurent was shaking.

Mrož smiled. He relaxed his grip on the gun and offered his palms.

"I saved my country! I saved it from itself. The Prague Spring made sense to me when it began. The party had ossified, and it needed change. But our leaders went too far. One morning, I woke up and realized the world had turned upside down. The movement, the reformers, the press, the writers, the artists ... they all wanted to eat my country from the inside out. Make it weak. Destroy its integrity."

"No, Janek, you've got it all wrong," Laurent said. Josie had surprised him with her outburst, the depth of her emotion. It gave him strength. "The people are your last hope."

"Look at them out there today, all the ones your age. Younger, even. For a short time, we let them listen to the Beatles. Now they are Beatles themselves, making chaos. No discipline. No respect for the work of the government or the goal of a better society. Where does it end?"

"In freedom," Laurent said. "What it takes to make a better world."

"And a new revolution," Josie added. "For everyone."

"That's the last thing I want."

Mrož picked up the phone. The unwavering note of the dial tone filled the room like a distant alarm. He put the receiver down on the desk, dialed a number, and lifted the receiver to his ear, all while keeping the barrel of the gun leveled at Josie and Laurent. He waited a moment, then spoke into the phone.

"Get me police headquarters, Commander Tesařová."

His voice, so cold, so decisive, struck Josie through with fear. She flashed back to the moment on the bridge when the Shrouded Man had leaped into the river. Now his body was sprawled on the floor.

Mrož was talking into the phone. Josie whispered to Laurent. "The Commander — she's the one who questioned me."

"The one with your papers?"

"Yes."

"Don't worry," Laurent said. "When she gets here, we'll explain. We're still members of the press."

"She won't take our side."

"Then we have to change Janek's mind."

Josie couldn't imagine that would work, the same as she couldn't imagine help from the police.

"Laurent, he's not the person you thought he was."

"I know how to engage him. He can't resist a good debate. It'll work."

"Just keep him talking. The troops outside were getting ready to move in. If they start before she arrives —"

Mrož hung up.

Laurent fixed his gaze on him. "Janek, where is Dubček?"

Mrož looked up at a clock.

"On his way to Moscow. He will be a special guest of the Kremlin. A Soviet delegation arrived this morning before the tanks to issue the invitation. He accepted."

"You mean they kidnapped him," Josie said.

"Call it what you like."

"The Soviets have had agents here for weeks, haven't they? Josie's right. They stole Dubček away, and you helped them."

"The movement had to be stopped. We need a strong government, not a weak one. The reformers had gained too much power in the Assembly and gone too far. The first step was to get the Soviets to come. It was easy. The second was to get rid of that fool Dubček."

"What about all the debates we had, Janek? About Kafka? Shakespeare? Camus? Carroll? What will happen to all those ideas when the Soviets take over? I'll tell you what'll happen. They'll be squelched. You're killing them."

"Literature has much to teach," Mrož said. "But what's the use if it teaches the wrong lessons? Like Carroll's nonsense, or Kafka's absurdity. They have no place in rational society. One that's ordered, predictable."

"You're wrong, Janek. Sometimes absurdity is the only rational response to the world around us."

"Kafka, whom you admire so much, wrote a story about a man who wakes up to find he's become a cockroach. The man doesn't know why. We don't know why. I doubt Kafka himself knew why. There was neither rhyme nor reason. What kind of a story is that? What does it teach us?"

Laurent recalled the students at Wenceslas Square, in particular the one who'd written the Russian word for "why" on the side of a tank.

"A truthful one, in a way," Laurent said. "But not fantastic enough. This morning your entire nation woke up to find itself stepped on, like a cockroach. Do you think the people understand why? Any reason you make up to justify it is as absurd as any story by Kafka or poem by Carroll."

"We were better off in the days Kafka was banned, before the Prague Spring. After that we traveled a road to ruin. I see it clearly now."

"The point of art isn't to bend people to its will, Janek. It's to set them free. What is it you're really afraid of?"

"Art that shows people the wrong way to live. That's a force too powerful to leave to chance. Fortunately, in the end, it's the one with the gun who decides. I'm sorry, but this is one debate I must win."

"I'll tell you what you're really afraid of. Not that books or music will set a bad example, but that they'll show people what's wrong with the world they already live in. Kafka wrote about horrors that came true, decades after he died. Authoritarianism. Censorship. Governments that operate in secret, their actions obscured from the people they serve. All of that's absurd. People aren't words to be set to meters and rhyme schemes. You've got to come clean. Tell people what you've done. Tell them it was a mistake. They love you, they'll understand."

"Enough!" Mrož's face contorted, made him ugly. "It doesn't matter now. Events have been set in motion. Unfortunately, now that you know my part in all this, I cannot let you leave."

Josie had listened while they debated, hoping Laurent's gamble on his friendship would work. Now she heard a commotion growing outside. The low growl of moving vehicles. Tense voices. Mrož had been too absorbed to notice. So had Laurent.

And he had failed. She had to try another tack.

"You called the police. How do you plan to explain to them why you murdered your aide?"

"Ah, the police. For the moment they remain useful, but they will soon be stripped of any power. I can't have you arrested by the Soviets, after all, can I? You, Miss Brouková, must be arrested by our own forces. As an enemy of the people."

The words hit Josie like a punch to the stomach. She drew in a breath and recovered herself. She saw it clearly, the scope of his ambitions. He had feet in both camps. He had leverage. He could rise to power with the outright support of the people, the tacit support of the Soviets, and no one aware that he'd engineered the ultimate betrayal.

"I know the Commander. She's sharp. She won't believe your lies."

"Josie hasn't done anything wrong," Laurent said. "Neither of us has."

"Haven't you?"

Mrož opened a drawer and pulled out another gun. He swapped it with the one he was holding and placed the first one on the desk.

"When the Commander and her forces arrive, they'll see not one dead body but three. I will, of course, be gutted with sorrow at such a horrible tragedy. However, I will muster the strength to explain. How the two of you, Western spies posing as reporters, threatened me. How my noble aide, a true patriot, ran to my defense, only to be shot by you. How I was able to call the police afterward but forced to kill you both — in self-defense — before they arrived."

Mrož stepped forward. His arm tensed. He straightened the barrel.

"No, Janek." Laurent's voice was barely audible.

Josie closed her eyes. She waited for the sound of the gun, for the shot at either her or Laurent. She didn't know which would be worse.

But the shot never came.

The Church

The building's foundation rumbled. Josie opened her eyes.

Mrož stared at the wall next to him. It shook, pebbles flying off. Then it burst open from floor to ceiling, showering debris. Bricks crumbled down, and the armored front edge of a tank broke through. A long, searching gun poked out and swung side to side, like the antenna of a massive insect. It kept coming and pushed the rest of the wall down, making a pile of rubble as tall as a person, dividing Josie and Laurent from Mrož.

Mrož yelled and fired his gun over the rubble. The tank advanced again, mindless, and it took him down. He was crushed beneath its treads.

Laurent and Josie traded expressions of horror and disbelief. They joined hands and ran from the office.

The Shrouded Man was dead. Mrož was dead.

Josie's source. Laurent's friend. *The traitor.*

But they were still in hot water.

Josie and Laurent ran through the cloud of dust and confusion hovering outside the Central Committee Building. They crossed the ruptured barricade and slipped between tanks.

Sirens blared. That would be the police, on their way, no doubt led by Commander Tesařová, to find the two foreigners alleged by Mrož to have killed an innocent, patriotic, Czech citizen.

And there would be no one to prove otherwise. No one except for the two of them, whom nobody would believe, because they'd been accused by a respected leader.

Overwhelmed by the shock, they found an alley off the square. They ducked inside and backed flat against the wall. Even so, they were barely hidden.

"Maybe we can evade them," Laurent said. "Run."

"But where?"

"Hotel. Embassy. I don't know."

"What about the radio network? We have to tell them what we know."

"There's no point going to the café."

Laurent peeked out of the alley. More people had entered the grand square since he and Josie had first arrived. The bigger-than-life figure of Jan Hus, burned as a heretic in 1415, stood solemnly at its center. Now squad cars pulled up at the corners, stopping along the Soviet vehicles already there. VB officers got out and joined the soldiers lining the cordons.

The noise of conflict that had been so ubiquitous all day long seemed distant now. All Laurent heard was the tinkling sound of chimes. He peered at the Old Town Hall across the square, and the clock that adorned it — the old astronomical clock, installed in the Middle Ages. Above it, the figures of apostles paraded behind little openings. A skeletal Death struck the hour. Vanity, Misery, and Lust shook their heads.

Legend had it that the city's fate was tied to that clock. Laurent wondered if the Soviets knew the legend, and if they would shoot it out to make a point. Or if they would remember that the Nazis had damaged it at the end of the war in 1945, but failed to quell an uprising.

Laurent watched two officers as they left a cordon and approached a couple of pedestrians, who dug into their pockets and produced booklets. The officers walked to another group nearby and did the same with them.

They were checking papers. They were focusing on young women. They were looking for one without identification. Josie.

"The streets are closed off," Laurent said. "We can't leave. They're stopping everyone."

Josie peeked out. Two officers stood at the next corner, facing the other way down the street. Across the plaza, a squad car skidded to a stop. An officer got out. Josie gasped.

"It's Tesařová. The Commander. I can't let her see me."

Laurent studied the woman in uniform. Her profile had the force and sharpness of a sword. Next to her stood a man with a bandage around his head.

"Oh no. Look who's with her."

The Commander was berating him: the State Security agent who'd tailed Josie, the one she'd clobbered to save Laurent's life. The Agent cowered while the Commander shouted.

"We could try to run for it."

"We might make it past some of the police, but —"

"Not all. I know."

"We need a better place to hide."

At the corner of the square stood an impressive baroque church. Josie watched as a handful of people walked out.

The government of Czechoslovakia was stuck in purgatory, but its churches — this one, at least — were still in business.

They waited until the Commander turned away and then rushed into the square, up the short steps, and through the decorated archway.

A priest in full vestments nodded at them. The whole church was a confessional today. Everyone given privacy. Everyone forgiven.

A few souls had come to pray. The nave was divided starkly between areas of light and dark. Sun filtered in through high windows to illuminate much of it, but shadows dominated the periphery, slithering like snakes over the stone, sitting thick in the corners like sleeping monsters.

At the far end of an aisle, Josie and Laurent took seats and bowed their heads. Josie felt a presence pervading the ancient structure, multiple presences, not the living. Silent echoes of past refugees, some of whom she guessed had not survived. She shivered.

The air was still. They sat nestled in what felt like a great stone vault, protected for the moment. But it was a vault that could trap them if they were discovered.

The enormity of what had happened rolled over both Josie and Laurent. They had been forced to run, with no time to think. Now they gave into the same emotional exhaustion. The same desperation. The same absence of hope. It drained away.

They reviewed their dismal state and came to the same conclusion. They'd learned a critical secret, but had no way to reach the people they needed to tell. Even if they knew where to go, they faced danger at every turn. They were journalists in a city under siege. They were wanted for murder. If they could make it out of the church alive, there was no guarantee they could reach safety — wherever that was.

Josie felt Laurent tense up.

"How does your shoulder feel?"

Laurent touched his wound.

"All that time. I couldn't see him for what he was. He fooled me."

"Laurent, he fooled everyone. He fooled the entire country."

"I can't help thinking, if I'd paid better attention, seen the signs. They must have been there."

She rested her head against his other shoulder.

"The Aide. He trusted me. That was my fault."

"No. He was killed by a sociopath. Not you."

Josie choked back a sob. Laurent understood. The gravity of the situation wasn't all they had in common. He saw how much she hungered for respect, how much she longed to figure out her place in the world. He put his arm around her, trying not to wince when he moved.

"And I was the one who told you to trust him."

Laurent looked up at the ornate ceiling and the crystal chandelier. Their beauty seemed like a cruel joke. They were meant to represent the expanse of Heaven, not a prison from which there was no escape. If Josie were not sitting there beside him —

Shouts came from the entrance. Josie and Laurent acted in unison, without exchanging a word. They scurried out of the row and positioned themselves behind a pillar at the end. Laurent put his face to the pillar and looked around it. He watched as two police officers wandered near the front, swinging nightsticks. They separated, and one started down the center aisle, preceded by a long shadow.

The other one came down the side aisle, straight toward their hiding place. Each strike of his heels against the marble floor thundered through the church like a cannon.

THE CRYPT

Laurent put his finger to his lips. Josie squeezed his hand.

They had seconds before the officer reached them. Josie looked around wildly. She crouched and crawled back into the pew.

Laurent saw why. The pillar would conceal them on this side, where the approaching officer was about to pass. Laurent crawled in beside her. They huddled together, their cheeks almost touching.

His footsteps receded. But now another set of boots approached. The other officer had finished a full pass along the other side of the church, and he was coming back down theirs.

As they waited, crouching, Josie thought of songs. Cheerful ones. "Penny Lane" came to mind, full of Paul McCartney's happy childhood memories. She let the melody drift between her ears. Laurent chose a poem to recite in his mind: "Jabberwocky." *'Twas brillig, and the slithy toves* ... The lines bounced and rolled. It was a lyrical poem with a happy ending. The vorpal sword gave him courage.

A voice rang out.

"Officers! How can I help you?"

It was the priest who'd welcomed Laurent and Josie in silence. He could be silent no longer.

"Have you seen a young woman? A foreigner?"

"I have seen many young people today. They are not in here. They are outside, doing their part against the invaders."

"This one is a criminal."

"Shame on you," the priest said, with the force of a trumpet. "You should be out there defending our country, not chasing young people into churches. There are no criminals here."

The priest's scolding left the officers dumbstruck. They didn't leave but sought out the chapels along the far side, which made more obvious hiding places.

Josie exhaled. Laurent smelled the fresh strawberry on her breath, still lingering from the café.

They peeked out together and saw the priest approach.

"Come, hurry," he whispered. He was old, weighted down by his garb. They followed him past the altar to a corridor with tiny chapels and a door. He struggled to open it, but it was jammed. Laurent helped, and it came unstuck. Creaking, it opened onto a set of stairs going down that led into a patch of darkness. The priest motioned them through.

"Follow the wall, my children. An exit leads up and out."

Laurent took his hand and shook it. Josie thanked him in Czech.

"In the last war, patriots hid here from the Nazis. They lost their lives. Take care that you do not."

They found themselves in a crypt below the church.

They ran their palms along the stone, brushing cobwebs. Things moved at their fingers and feet. But rats and spiders were nothing compared to gun-wielding men or tanks that ran into buildings.

Josie found the way out first and reached for the door.

"Wait," Laurent said. "Where are we going?"

"To find the other members of the secret network, of course. We have to tell them what we know."

"We caught a break here. But half the city's police are still out hunting for you."

Josie pictured the scene inside the café after they'd left, what it must look like now. The windows would be dark. No sign of life. Tables and chairs on their sides. Dishes strewn and broken, shards of glass everywhere. In the room upstairs, radio equipment smashed, panels pulled open, wires ripped out.

She refused to picture bodies, bruised on their heads or wounded by shots to their chests. She hoped fervently against those thoughts.

"This is more important than me," she said.

"You're in danger. Who knows what they'll do to you. Arrest you? Turn you over to the Soviets? They'll use you, blame you, call you a liar."

"We have to find out who the other conspirators are, the men who invited this invasion."

"The invasion would've taken place with or without them."

"I know. But the Playwright, her people, they have to know who they can trust. We have to help them. You said so yourself."

Laurent could tell Josie believed what she was saying, deeply. He knew it was the right thing to do. And he wanted to stay by her side. But the priest's warning had spooked him. He felt responsible for her safety.

"*We* can't do anything right now. You have to get out of the country. Mrož may be dead, but his ghost will see you to prison."

"*We* can't? What do you mean, *we* can't?"

"They aren't after me."

"Wait a minute. You're in danger too. People have seen us together. They'll put two and two together, and then —"

"Only one person who knows about this has seen us together — the Agent. The Commander seems to have him on a tight leash. That means I have time. I can try my contacts. They can get word to the secret network, tell them what Mrož and his collaborators have done, that Dubček is innocent."

"And what am I supposed to do? Stay here in hiding?"

"You have no time. You have to get to the Hotel International, fast. The Americans are organizing a convoy to leave the country. They have room for us. I'll meet you there."

"You forget, I have no papers. I can't cross the border."

"They're taking Czechs who need discretion and a way out. They can take you."

She recalled the Commander's threat. *You are nothing but a girl who speaks Czech in the middle of an invasion of a country you cannot leave.* She couldn't stay here, but she couldn't go anywhere else. The police would expect her to try the bureau. Or the Canadian embassy. No. Laurent was being sensible.

And the police weren't after him — as long as he wasn't with her. But he would still be taking a risk. And any attempt to contact the radio operators could get them in trouble too.

A silence came between them. There were so many unasked questions. So many unshared stories.

"Go to your contacts," Josie said. "Get the word out. But promise me, as soon as you're done, you'll come to the hotel. Don't be long."

"I will. But promise me, if I don't make it there before the convoy leaves, you'll go without me. Ask for an American named Freddy. Tell him I sent you."

"That won't be necessary. Just make it there."

They opened the door and squinted at the daylight. When their eyes adjusted, they walked up the crumbling steps to a street behind the church, outside the square. There were no police.

Laurent stopped. Josie stepped forward and wrapped her arms around him. They held on for a moment, then went their separate ways.

Josie wondered if she would ever see him again.

The Chase

Laurent knew right away he had to break his promise.

The contacts he had in mind were nearby, in the old part of Prague, and he found one quickly. The man said he would try to pass on the information, without any guarantee. But as soon as he left, Laurent knew he had one more thing to do. And it meant he couldn't go to the hotel to meet Josie. Not yet.

He knew that if he'd told her what he wanted to do, she would have objected, and she would have refused to go on without him. So he'd had no choice.

He was going to save her. He was going to make sure she made it out of the country alive.

The police believed that Josie had murdered a popular leader's trusted aide. They might even hold her responsible for the death of Mrož, someone who might have led them through a nightmare. She was public enemy number one. The police might be powerless against the heavy artillery of the Soviets, but she made a perfect scapegoat. They were going to scour the city until they found her.

Laurent had to make sure they didn't. He was going to lead them away from Josie. Away from the Hotel International. Away from the convoy, which Laurent hoped would soon be making its way south toward Davle and Austria, with Josie on board.

He had to give the police a reason to believe, for the moment, that she wasn't leaving Prague.

But for a time he wandered, unable to figure out how to achieve that end. How to distract Josie's pursuers. He couldn't concentrate. Then he remembered the advice he had given Josie when she couldn't remember details about the Shrouded Man.

Stop trying. Think about something else.

He thought about her. How they'd kept bumping into each other, like they were destined to meet. Each time they'd seemed out of sync. One coming, the other going. Finally, their separate missions had merged.

Now they shared a purpose. But once again, events had sent them in different directions.

What was the song Josie had mentioned at the Slavia?

Hello, Goodbye.

She'd never had the chance to explain it.

A squad car whizzed by. Laurent ducked behind a stalled bus. Another one passed, filled with officers. Watching them, he almost bumped into a police officer on the street. There were so many there.

Laurent realized that the whole time, without thinking about it, he'd been walking toward the place where his day had begun.

It was the place where it made the most sense for him to go, but at the same time it was the place where he could least afford to be seen. The most logical, the most absurd, and the most dangerous.

Police headquarters.

While Josie rushed to leave her pursuers behind, Laurent was headed straight for them.

Hello. Goodbye.

He came up with a plan in less than a minute.

He found a shop and asked for a telephone, saying he needed to make an urgent call and stressing that he needed privacy. The shopkeeper showed him to a back room. Laurent noted that he had piqued the man's curiosity. Beneath the chaos and conflict, paranoia was working its way through Prague, fed by uncertainty and fear. Laurent didn't like it, but he could use it to his advantage.

The shopkeeper left him alone but kept the door ajar and lingered outside, making noises at the counter that too obviously signaled he was trying to go about his business. Laurent picked up the telephone receiver and pretended to dial a number. He made sure to cup his hand over the receiver in a way that seemed suspicious, but at the same time allowed him to talk loud enough for the shopkeeper to hear. He was tempted to glance up and confirm the man was paying attention. But that might scare him off. He had to trust his plan.

"Josefina," he said, using the Czech version of Josie's name. The shopkeeper would hear it and remember it. "The police are after you. They know what you did. They know you shot and killed Janek Mrož's aide, that you tried to kill Mrož too. I overheard them, and they were saying your name over and over again, Brouková, Brouková, Brouková. You have to meet me on Vitkov Hill. That's right, Vitkov Hill. Hurry."

Laurent hung up. The noise from the store counter had stopped. It meant the shopkeeper had been listening. That he'd been transfixed.

Laurent ran from the shop. Outside, he stopped at the edge of the window. The shopkeeper went into the back room. He picked up the phone.

He was calling the police.

It had worked.

But Laurent had to make sure. He found another shop nearby and went inside to wait. He pretended to browse the shelves. Police headquarters was around the corner and down the next block. Vitkov Hill was west of here. If they got the message and acted on it, they would pass right outside.

Ten minutes went by. Half an hour. He got worried. There was no sign of a police mobilization. Had they put out a call to another station closer to the hill? Or radioed officers who were already there?

It wouldn't be enough. Police command had to get involved. Laurent wanted to increase attention where he directed it, so they couldn't search elsewhere.

He would have to use himself as bait.

He walked the short distance to Bartolomějská Street. He turned the corner, and there it was: the tiled and windowed facade of the place where citizens went in and often never came out.

He watched from behind a van across the street. The station was a hive of activity, buzzing with voices, motors, and sirens. He would have to make himself seen, but not yet. He had to wait for the perfect moment. He hoped it would come soon. He was terrified.

A man in a long coat emerged from the station. He had a bandage on his head.

The Agent, here. Laurent's heart knotted into a fist.

Their nemesis still had the same expression that Laurent had seen flash across his face outside the church, when Commander Tesařová had turned away after scolding him. Hatred. Laurent knew why. He knew who'd clobbered him, and he'd let her go. Josie had humiliated him.

This man had no intention of arresting her, no matter what the Commander or anyone else said.

He was going to find her and kill her.

A wave of emotion overwhelmed Laurent. If Josie died today, it would be worse than if he died himself.

A sputtering motor brought him back to his surroundings. An officer rode by on a motorcycle. He pulled up alongside the station, then jumped off and walked away, leaving it idling.

The bike's blue and white shell gleamed. It was a model made for the Czechoslovak police, a Jawa "Nanuk" with a fast 344cc engine. It called out to Laurent.

This was the moment.

He walked toward the machine. There was a lot going on, and the Agent hadn't seen him. He picked up his pace. A clearing opened around the motorcycle.

He broke into a run and leaped onto the seat. He grabbed the handlebars, kicked the stand, and pulled the clutch.

Then he revved the engine and drove at the Agent like a bull at a target. When he saw the recognition dawn, Laurent swerved and sped off.

Shouts and whistles came from behind. A siren. Seconds later, two squad cars joined pursuit.

The rearview mirror showed police in tow. Laurent leaned into a sharp turn and stole a glance over his shoulder. What he saw there astonished him.

At the head of the column of squad cars was another motorcycle, bigger than Laurent's, all black metal. The Agent was on it, gripping the handlebars like weapons. He wore monstrous goggles. Smoke from the exhaust rose behind him like wings made of coal.

He rode at Laurent like an angel of death.

THE SONG

All You Need Is Love.

Someone had chalked the words on the side of a disabled tank that was spewing smoke.

Was it true? Josie didn't know, but she ached to hear the song, the final track from her *Magical Mystery Tour* LP. The Beatles had sung it as a worldwide appeal for peace and harmony, in the simplest, most joyful way possible. They'd performed it live via satellite last year and reached hundreds of millions of people with their message, a global connection that was unprecedented.

Right now, Josie wanted to hear it for comfort. The memory of the Aide cut away at her insides. She grieved in a way she couldn't explain. The song couldn't change what had already happened, but it could be a salve for her pain. It rang out in her imagination, beginning with its bright, hopeful rendition of "La Marseillaise," the French national anthem. That made her think of Laurent.

She hummed the tune out loud as she walked, and it lent her strength. She repeated it, then proceeded backward through the other tracks on the album. "Baby You're a Rich Man." "Penny Lane." "Strawberry Fields Forever."

Strawberry fields.

It came back to Josie in a flash: the clatter of dishes, the Beatles playing on the speakers, the bowl of fresh berries. The Café Skrýš, which might never serve customers again. The words the waiter had spoken: *The strawberries are still growing there. It's a miracle.* They'd come from a farm in the village of Jahodová Pole, south of Prague.

And the words of the Playwright soon after — about locations where the new resistance was setting up its network of secret radio stations.

In stables, attics, kitchens, farmhouses. In these places, hope springs like a miracle.

The strawberry farm in Jahodová Pole was one of the stations. She knew it now, but it was too late. She had to get to the convoy.

A shadow fell across her. The Hotel International loomed ahead.

By the time Josie walked in, there was no sign of any convoy or film crew. She found an American, a young man with horn-rimmed glasses and short hair, pacing the lobby with a clipboard.

He was a consular officer from their embassy. He said the convoy had come and gone.

"But they're organizing a second convoy. Are you with the crew? You can wait."

"When does it leave?"

"Not long. A couple of hours."

Josie slumped. By that time, the hotel might be swarming with police. There could be Soviet agents searching for her too, like the ones who'd ransacked the café. Either Czechoslovak police or Soviet troops could burst through the hotel entrance at any time. It was a matter of minutes, not hours.

"What route is the convoy taking to Austria?"

"South along the river and west to the border."

"Are they making stops?"

"As a matter of fact, yes. They're picking up the rest of the film crew along the way. They're stranded. All they've got are military trucks they rented from Austria, and they can't very well drive across the country in those. The Soviets have already said the movie was cover for an invasion by the West."

"Where are they?"

"Davle."

"Have you ever heard of Jahodová Pole? Do you know if it's near Davle?"

"Yes." He raised an eyebrow. "It's the next town over."

"Thank you."

Josie could find someone to drive her and head for Davle. The convoy would travel slowly. She could make it in time.

Or she could go to Jahodová Pole first, and try to warn the radio resistance.

One way would put her on the path to Austria, and safety. Over the border, away from the forces that pursued her.

The other way promised nothing. She might be wrong and still miss the convoy. She couldn't be certain she would even find the secret broadcasters in Jahodová Pole, or that they would listen if she did. But if by chance she was right, and she was able to warn Radio Free Czechoslovakia, she could still try to get to Davle in time.

Josie's leg cramped up. Space was tight in the trunk of the small car that concealed her, and the road out of Prague was bumpy. She was grateful to the driver — he was a hotel employee anxious to get to his family in the country — but she wished he drove a bigger car.

The latch on the trunk was loose, so when the car slowed down at intersections, Josie could open it to peek out. Headless posts dotted the intersections. Josie guessed that ordinary people had removed the names from the signs like in the city, defending by obfuscation. But not all the place names were gone. One destination remained on the signs, and they all pointed east: Moscow. An unsubtle hint to the armored cars and troop transports that rolled roughshod over roads in the opposite direction.

Josie tried to work out what mattered most, and why. She wanted to report on the invasion and break the story she'd discovered. Her calling as a journalist was important. But she also wanted respect, from her fellow journalists, her editors, her family. There was her babička, whom she'd thought more about in a single day than in the last few months. The memories had grown more vivid, and Josie missed her babička more than ever. And now there was the urgency of delivering information to the new resistance. Finally, there was Laurent. She didn't understand why he wanted to protect her, or why she trusted him. All the rest of it seemed to strengthen their bond, as if the pieces of a puzzle had fallen together.

There was no clear winner as to what mattered most. All the parts overlapped and interlocked, and she couldn't tease them apart.

Most of all, Josie thought about the Aide. Maybe Laurent was right. Maybe she wasn't responsible all by herself. But she'd played a part in his death, and it shook her. What had he been like? Did he have a family? In the morning, he'd been a man without a face, but even now, he still had no name. She wished she knew it. She didn't want to remember him by a shadowy moniker that said more about his death than about his life.

The car stopped. Josie listened for the sound of the running engine to go quiet.

It kept running. She waited.

Footsteps came on the gravel, behind the car. And a shout — not the driver. She couldn't make out the words, but she was pretty certain they weren't Czech or Slovak.

The footsteps passed and stopped at the front. She heard the driver talking. He sounded hurried and nervous. The other voice asked curt questions. Now the other man was speaking Czech, but with an accent.

"Where are you going?"

"To Davle, sir."

"Davle! And why are you going there?"

"It is … my family's home in the country."

Josie hoped he'd be believed. He sounded on the verge of breaking down. Her heart pounded.

"How much farther is it?"

"Um … two or three kilometers. We are almost there."

"Is this also the road to Jahodová Pole? Your infernal country has no signs!"

Josie's hope fell like a weight. They knew about the secret radio station.

"Yes, sir. Jahodová Pole is not far. It comes before Davle."

"Good. Once you get to Davle, stay there. Roadblocks are going up tonight. We do this for your sake. Your countrymen are only making it more difficult, you know. And they are only making things worse for themselves."

Josie heard the officer's footsteps as he walked away from the driver. Then they stopped and went back to the front of the car.

The officer spoke again. This time he was more pointed, tense.

"You said *we* are almost there. What did you mean?"

Josie's blood froze.

THE HILL

The cobblestones of Old Town ensured a rough ride. Laurent took a chance and turned down an alley. The plastic housing around the front of the motorcycle scraped against the walls on either side. But it paid off — he came to a boulevard, which would carry him faster and farther. He had to keep the police in pursuit as long as he could, even if it meant going in circles.

Laurent headed for a park west of downtown, on Vitkov Hill. Mrož had told him about it once and shown him the way, and Laurent had gone again for its beautiful vistas. He remembered the route. The footpaths leading up were closed to road traffic, but on a motorcycle he could navigate the paths and lose the squad cars.

The chase to Vitkov Hill took fifteen minutes, straining the muscles in Laurent's arms and testing his will. His shoulder ached. He tried to push the pain away and concentrated on the path. He swerved around a row of tanks and dodged a fiery barricade. For a short time, he seemed to have lost the police. But the string of squad cars reappeared, the devilish Agent at their front, and soon they were a short distance behind him.

Laurent left the boulevard and chose small streets with sharp curves. A squad car failed to manage a hairpin and collided with a streetlamp. Laurent had to slow down to approach the hill, and his pursuers closed in. As soon as he saw the footpath at the foot of Vitkov Hill, he throttled the engine and burst forward. The cars screeched to a halt at the bottom, but the Agent roared on behind him. Laurent saw him in the mirror, coming up at a ferocious speed.

Laurent raced faster and faster up the hill, circling toward the top. He'd been so crazy with worry and panic over Josie that he'd only worked out the beginning of his plan, not the end.

In a minute, he'd be at the top. And he'd be trapped.

The road burst through clumps of trees on either side and opened onto a plateau surrounded by a breathtaking panorama. The top of the hill, and the end of the line. In the middle of a grand plaza stood a huge stone memorial with a statue of a Czech hero on horseback. Laurent raced around it and skidded to a stop. He leaped off the motorcycle. Uncertain what else to do, he ran. Twenty feet from the edge of the overlook, he stopped, out of breath.

The Agent pulled up and dismounted.

"You," he snarled, "have a punishment coming. You and your friend. Where is she?"

"She's meeting me here."

"Not anymore," the Agent said. He pulled the gun from his holster and waved it. "It is I she will meet here. You, she will find dead."

The noise of an engine spitting and popping interrupted him. Another motorcycle approached, a "Nanuk" like Laurent's, but with a sidecar attached.

Both the driver and the occupant of the sidecar wore goggles like the Agent's. The driver stayed put, but the woman in uniform next to him pulled hers off and got out of the sidecar. She had a face like a blade and medals on her jacket. Laurent recognized Commander Tesařová, because Josie had pointed her out in Old Town Square.

The Agent stomped his foot in frustration. Laurent watched the Commander approach them.

"Lower your gun, Agent."

"But —"

"Do as you're told. That kind of behavior is for the Soviets, not us. We want answers, not dead suspects."

Josie had said the Commander was sharp. A glimmer of hope surfaced. But Josie had also been frightened by her. Now that the Commander was here, Laurent didn't know what to expect.

"I will take care of this," she instructed the Agent. "Go back to your bike and radio headquarters. Tell them we have one and will soon have the other."

Laurent felt a thrill. He remained in danger, but his plan seemed to be working. He had drawn the fire from Josie.

Now, however, he stood face-to-face with a danger all his own.

"Miss Brouková is a friend of yours?"

Laurent nodded. The Commander's eyes burned.

"For the second time in a single day, this extraordinary day, she has drawn out half the police in Prague. But I am afraid her time is up."

"What you've been told about Josie isn't true," Laurent said. He hadn't planned to explain the truth to the police, any of it. But now, facing the Commander, he could not hold back.

"Whoever you are," she said, "I advise you to stay out of this. My concern is Miss Brouková, not you."

"I won't abandon her."

"Suit yourself. But tell me, did she find the man from the bridge?"

Laurent swallowed hard.

"She did."

"Who is he?"

"If I tell you, you're not going to like it."

"Try me."

"He was an aide to Janek Mrož."

"Was?"

"He's dead now."

"The one she killed."

"No! Mrož shot him. And he meant to shoot us too."

The Commander was taken aback.

"Why would he do that?"

"This morning on the bridge, that aide tried to give Josie a message. That's why Mrož shot him. Mrož has been working with the Soviets. He confessed to us. He belonged to a group of party officials who wrote to the Kremlin and urged them to come to Prague with all their military might. Their letter was printed in newspapers across the Eastern bloc this morning, but with no signatures."

"Lies," the Commander said. She drew a pistol. But she no longer seemed as certain as she had moments ago. Laurent sensed a hesitation. An opportunity.

"I've known Josie for one day. No longer than you have. But I know her well enough, and I think you do too. You questioned her. You looked in her eyes. Do you really think she did this?"

"I gather your friend is not coming."

Laurent said nothing.

"You went to a great deal of trouble to bring us here."

"I did what I had to."

The Agent had returned. He stood listening. "You cannot possibly believe this man," he said.

Laurent tried to decipher the Commander's expression. It was inscrutable.

"As a matter of fact, I do."

The Agent gaped. "Are you insane? They are enemies of the state!"

"Yes," the Commander replied. "But which state?"

She raised her gun at the Agent and shouted in Czech to the officer who'd driven her. He came over and clapped handcuffs onto the Agent's wrists. The Agent struggled and spewed what Laurent guessed were vile curses.

"He is overzealous," the Commander said. "And I suspect working for them already. Is he responsible for that wound on your shoulder?"

Laurent touched the spot. It smarted.

"I consider myself an excellent judge of character," she told him. "And my conscience tells me to believe you. There's an old Czech expression: A fish rots from the head. This whole business smelled rotten from the start. Now I understand how rotten."

An immense weight lifted from Laurent.

"Weeks ago, there were rumors of a planned coup, to topple Dubček." A jet roared overhead. The Commander paused until it passed. "State Security has orders to find and arrest Miss Brouková. I cannot reverse them. I do not even know who is in charge anymore. For the moment, however, I can look the other way. I can tell you to run. I do not expect to have this job much longer, but I will not assist the efforts of a traitor, dead or alive. The Soviets are not calling *all* the shots yet."

She raised her handheld radio. She pressed a button on the side, and it crackled.

"Our suspect has left the area. Move east and continue the search."

She put it back on her belt.

"Some may roll over for the Soviets. But I will not. Now get out of Prague. Leave Czechoslovakia and go home. I expect Miss Brouková is already headed for the border. When you see her, give her these."

The Commander pulled out a half-size manila envelope. Laurent took it and slid out Josie's passport and press card. He didn't tell her it was too late.

"Thank you."

She walked back to the motorcycles. Her driver put the Agent in the sidecar. She got on the other bike, and they rode off.

Laurent walked the remaining distance to the edge of the overlook. He stood there and took in the view of Prague, the city whose people and history he'd gotten to know so well over the past year. He would miss them. The scene spread out before him: river, bridges, steeples, rooftops. All that was ordinary, and all that was extraordinary. All that was beautiful, and all that was ugly.

If only society could be as beautiful and orderly as a sonnet.

Mrož had said that, it seemed, so long ago, when he'd been alive, when they'd been friends. When he cared more about beauty than about order. When he cared more for his people than for power.

Society was not a sonnet, and it never would be.

Laurent loved poetry's economy, its power to convey images and to fill the mind with sensation. Every word counted. It was like the spare style he'd learned for newspaper writing, which had a power of its own if not the same beauty. Poetry had always provided Laurent a refuge. But a poem was not a prescription for human behavior. A poem was an unfathomable mystery.

Laurent had always known a poem could be a mystery. Now, thanks to Josie, he knew a song could too.

Laurent looked to the left, southward. Somewhere out there, Josie was making her way to freedom.

He held tightly onto her papers. It was too late for them to do any good. But he told himself that as long as he held on to them and kept them safe, she'd be safe too. One day soon, he would return them to her.

The Farm

Josie nudged open the lid of the trunk, just an inch. She dreaded the sound it might make. But she had to see for herself what was going on. Luckily, no sound came.

She squinted through the crack at the harsh rays of the sun, now low on the horizon. A jeep was parked behind them. It had Soviet markings — a red star and the letters *CCCP*. Beyond it sat a covered truck that was olive green. In addition to the driver of the truck, she saw the helmeted heads of soldiers leaning out.

Off the road, thirty feet away, stood a thick crop of trees at the bottom of a slope.

She was about to be discovered. She knew it in her gut. If she made no move, she could be captured, taken back to Prague, arrested. Or worse. She might never get out of Czechoslovakia. Or they might take her out across the wrong border, east to the Soviet side.

But would she even make it that far? Would they shoot her right here, by the side of the road?

Whether they discovered her or not, the radio broadcasters in Jahodová Pole were in danger. She knew the Soviets meant to destroy their operation and silence their voices, no matter what it took. And the bond to this land and its people that had been growing within her could not allow it — no matter what it took.

Josie braced herself. With all the power she could muster she kicked at the trunk. It shot open, and she leaped out of the car and ran for the trees.

She did not look back or hesitate. Shouts came, and gunfire. She knew soldiers were jumping from the truck to pursue her. A wide ditch opened at the bottom of the slope, before the woods. A stream ran through it. She jumped over, carried by the momentum of her downward speed. The memory of the Shrouded Man — Mrož's poor aide, jumping from the bridge, getting shot — flashed through her mind. She ran into the woods.

A car squealed. She knew the sound: her driver, racing away. She hoped he made it, wherever he was going.

But in the next second, a blast thundered from the road. Out of the corner of her eye, she saw smoke rise and flames lick the sky. The driver's decision to run had been the wrong one. Josie fought back tears.

And now they turned their attention back to her. Bullets rattled the air. They thudded into trees. Running feet trampled the ground behind her. The noise sounded like it was all around her, right up close.

But the forest had amplified the noise. They were far behind. The forest was thick, full of dense undergrowth and covered by a heavy canopy, and getting darker. She was smaller, light-footed, unencumbered.

She ran and ran. Soon she no longer heard her pursuers. Had they given up? No — they'd gone back to their transport, to take the road to Jahodová Pole. Josie couldn't see past her immediate wooded surroundings, but she could picture the winding river and the rolling hills around it. The road had to follow the curves of the terrain, and so did the soldiers. She could get to Jahodová Pole first if she ran fast.

She had to. The Soviets would tear the town apart. If the station was there, they would find it. She had to find the strawberry farm and warn the Playwright's confederates.

But where was it? Josie knew the town was situated on this side of the river. The driver had said they were close. And as soon as she'd gone deep enough into the forest, she'd headed to the right, the direction they'd been traveling on the road. But it didn't matter how fast she ran. Without better knowledge, she'd run right past the town and miss the farm.

She slowed down and stopped. She bent over, panted, caught her breath. Every muscle was drained, her spirit defeated. All she could do was listen to the sounds of the forest. A stream trickled in the distance.

Its peaceful bubbling percolated with the quality of music. It seemed to echo a melody, which she recognized as "Strawberry Fields Forever." Laurent had been right: Their music followed her. This song had always calmed her and reassured her, especially when she'd felt uncertain about her path, when she'd felt most alone.

She'd never felt more alone than she did right now.

She found an old tree with branches low enough to gain a foothold. She didn't have to climb the whole way up, just high enough to catch a glimpse of the countryside. "Strawberry Fields Forever" played on in her head.

Josie knew the song had been inspired by a childhood memory, a place John Lennon had known in Liverpool. Like all children, he had climbed trees, and in the song there was a line about being in one, all alone, looking out at the world. No one saw the world in quite the same way he did. But that was all right. It's what made him special. It's what made anyone — everyone — special in their own way. Your memories, where you came from, the way you looked at the world. It was the place you had to be before you got to where you were going.

Bark scraped Josie's arms as she scurried up the trunk. She had to squeeze through a tight opening between branches. She lost her grip once and slipped, burning her thighs. Halfway to the top, a gap opened in the canopy, and she scanned the valley. Not far away, tucked inside a bend in the river, she spotted a collection of rooftops. On the near side lay an open field. A farm.

Josie thought to herself, *I can make it.*

She tumbled all the way down, then broke once more into a sprint, this time in a new direction. Her adrenaline surged. Trees whipped at her face. She no longer heard the sound her feet made trampling leaves and crushing twigs — all she heard was the rushing in her ears.

The forest fell away, and a vast field appeared. On elevated ground sat a farmhouse with a barn surrounded by rusted heavy machinery.

Josie stopped. Out front was an old, damaged tractor and a small cart laden with bushels. They contained strawberries.

This was it.

Josie ran on. The windows in the farmhouse were dark. She went to the barn instead, where a light flickered. Inside, a ladder led up to a loft. She mounted the rungs one by one until she reached the top, and peeked through the opening.

Three people sat at a table, huddled around a radio. An old man dipped his head to a mic and breathed into its grille. A young woman was pointing to lines in a notebook, angled for the old man to see. The third person, a young man, operated the transmitter.

Josie jumped up and waved her arms. Two of the renegade broadcasters, startled, reacted in the ways they'd practiced. The young man spun a dial and hit switches. The woman drew matches from her purse, intended for the notebook. But the old man merely swiveled toward Josie, curious about her intrusion.

Breathlessly, she spoke to them in Czech.

"Soviets are coming. They know you're here. You must run!"

They didn't need to hear more. The young couple jumped to their feet and took their elder by his arms.

As they climbed down, Josie told them in clipped sentences about the raid on the Café Skrýš and what Mrož had done.

"You were right to find us," the woman said. "We are grateful. But you must be mistaken about Mrož. He would not do that."

Josie fought the urge to argue. The Soviets might arrive at any moment. The broadcasters had to get out of Jahodová Pole, and she had to find the convoy.

The broadcasters jumped into a truck parked on the other side of the barn. The old man beckoned to Josie.

"I can't come with you."

He said, "You are leaving Czechoslovakia?"

"I don't want to. I have to."

"Tell the world," he said. "Tell them about our brave children. Tell them how we stood up."

Before she could say another word, they raced away.

She smiled at the thought that she had helped them escape the Aide's fate — for their own sakes, and for their country's. In the days ahead, the people of Czechoslovakia would be denied freedom, and they would be denied the truth. They would need all the strength and support they could muster. The clandestine radio network would provide a foundation.

Josie took in the vista before her. Rows of green bushes stretched across the fields. Forever, it seemed. She thought she saw a small girl in pigtails skipping through the field. Had she imagined it? Had her grandmother looked like that as a child, when she'd played between the rows?

Yes, this was the farm where the strawberries were still growing, out of season, like a miracle.

But that's not all it was.

It was her babička's farm. Not as lush as in her stories, as it had been before the communists collectivized the farms. But Josie was certain. Like Laurent had predicted.

Her stories live in me.

A red sun set over blue mountains in the distance. Josie reflected on the long day: the people she'd met, the thrills and the dangers, and now her arrival at the magical place she had dreamed about since childhood. She forgot the cramp in her leg. She had traveled half the world away from Toronto, but the sensation welling up inside her told her she'd finally come home.

Home could mean more than a place. It could be a feeling.

But there was one part missing. One person. To get to him, she could no longer run back. She had to run forward, and hope that he did too.

She would have to trust him.

Away from home, not even certain what home meant anymore, Josie had found herself in the middle of the biggest story she had ever encountered. But there was a story within the story, and a song within that, which no one else knew about except for her and Laurent.

A desire welled up inside her. It was the urge to seek out the hidden stories in the world, and all its unheard people, and to give them a voice. Wherever she found them, she would call that home.

On the far side of the field, past where the strawberries seemed to go on forever, a line of trucks appeared, coming around a bend in the road. They were not military, Soviet or otherwise. It was the convoy, heading for the border.

Josie could make it if she flew like the wind.

She jumped into the field and ran down the neat lines of small green bushes flecked with tiny red fruits. Like her babička, she ran, and she laughed as she ran, like she was a child again in a place where she had never been.

Epilogue

A light rain fell on the Left Bank as Josie made her way through the narrow streets. She had no umbrella — only the map she'd acquired at the train station. She held it over her head as she crossed Rue Dauphine. She was looking for a café.

Three months had passed since her escape from Czechoslovakia. At the border, the Americans had concealed her in the back of a truck. When they crossed, the guards had barely checked passports, but State Security officers had been on hand searching with their eyes.

As soon as Josie had arrived in Austria, she'd found a telephone and called the news desk in Toronto. She'd furiously dictated the notes she'd scribbled on the journey south, and her report appeared on her paper's front page the next morning. She recounted the struggles, frustrations, and heroics of the city's nonviolent resistance.

Instead of bringing her home, her editors asked her to remain in Vienna so she could continue to report on the Soviet occupation from there. Vienna proved a useful place to be. In spite of the rumors that had begun the first day of the invasion, the Soviet occupiers did not close the borders until months later, and thousands of refugees fled the country. Many went to the Austrian capital, and they maintained connections to friends and family at home for as long as they could.

For weeks Josie heard nothing of Laurent's fate. He had no byline on the front page of *Paris Flash*, but she was certain that many of the words were his — his voice echoed out of them. She assumed he hadn't made it out of Prague that day, but her repeated inquiries to his paper went unanswered. She couldn't guess what had happened to him, and it worried her immensely. Was he still there, in hiding? Had he not been able to leave? Had he been arrested?

The news she awaited came one evening. Returning from a long day after tracking down a pair of Slovak writers and interviewing a Soviet diplomat, she found a message waiting at the hotel front desk.

IN TRANSIT TO PARIS. MEET ME? LAURENT

He was in West Berlin, and he'd left a number. She tried to reach him, and he tried her back, but they only communicated by messages left with hotel clerks. They agreed on a date, and Josie arranged for travel to Paris by a succession of trains.

She couldn't contain her excitement as she disembarked at Gare de l'Est. But outside the café, she waited before going in. She reflected on the last time she'd looked through windows like these, Laurent standing beside her.

She knew the decision to walk through this door, like the last one, would change her life.

Laurent sat there with a newspaper he hadn't yet opened. He tapped his fingers and darted looks everywhere at once. When he saw Josie, he waved at her with an enormous smile on his face, standing up with such fervor that his chair fell backward into the customer behind him, spilling her coffee.

Their embrace in the middle of the crowded café, filled with more patrons than it had chairs for, delayed orders and hindered the progress of waitresses. Josie and Laurent remained oblivious

— until a rousing applause alerted them once again to the presence of the rest of the world. Josie blushed. Laurent smiled warmly. When they took their seats, a song came on the radio: "Dear Prudence," a track from the Beatles' newly released White Album.

It was a song, Josie explained to Laurent, about bravery, hope, and renewal.

They held hands across the tiny table and shared the pain and exultation that still remained from that last day in Prague. But their conversation moved to the present, and then the future, and they remained at the café until well past dark, only leaving when it closed.

In the days afterward, Josie had to return to Vienna. Almost immediately, she persuaded her editors to assign her to an opening in the paper's Paris bureau.

They married the following year. Not long after, Josie gave birth to a feisty infant who kicked her way out into the world. Her parents named her for the song playing on the radio in the Paris café.

It was a brand new day. Josie and Laurent lived and worked in Paris for the early years of their daughter's life, and then they traveled with her across Europe as foreign correspondents. They had every reason to be happy, and were ambitious in their careers. But for two people so young, their experiences in Prague had left scars that were not easily erased. The tragedies they'd witnessed on that tumultuous day never faded from their memories.

Laurent still mourned the friendship that had ended in betrayal and violence. He questioned his judgment and worried about his capacity to trust, but he worked hard to restore his faith in the fundamental goodness of people. He spent years, as a reporter, husband, and father, building it back.

Josie never forgot the Aide. His memory haunted her for years. She vowed that he would not go nameless, and that one day she would tell his story. Josie pursued the quest whenever she could. The Soviet occupation had sent a diaspora of Czechs and Slovaks far and wide, and she peppered expatriates with questions wherever she found them, seeking to discover the Aide's name and any information they could reveal. Little by little, she accumulated details. But the Aide's identity, and his story, seemed lost forever.

More than a decade later, on a park bench in Latvia, she wrested the crucial answer from a man who had known him. Finally, Josie learned the Aide's name, and she could tell his story.

HISTORICAL NOTE

One week after the fateful invasion on August 21, 1968, the free radio network broadcast the voice of Czechoslovakia's beloved leader, Alexander Dubček. He was emotionally drained. The Soviets had kidnapped him and taken him to Moscow, and now he had returned, thanks to monumental efforts by his peers.

He could barely speak, but his message was clear: the too-short Prague Spring was over. In spite of the heroic protests of tens of thousands of Czechs and Slovaks, young and old, the Soviets had won. New restrictions were enforced. Freedom was relegated the past. A curtain of darkness fell over the nation, silencing all but the bravest voices. The clandestine radio stations disappeared from the airwaves.

On August 26, the Beatles released a new song: "Revolution," the B-side of the single "Hey Jude." It became an anthem for many Czechoslovaks, played in secret by an underground movement that worked for two decades to lead the country to freedom.

A playwright, like the fictional one Josie and Laurent encounter above the Café Skrýš, joined the movement. In 1989, he became a leader of the Velvet Revolution, which finished what the Prague Spring had begun. After twenty years under a repressive regime installed by the Soviet Union, it secured freedom and self-determination for the people of Czechoslovakia. The playwright's name was Vaclav Havel, and the newly empowered people of Czechoslovakia elected him president.

Journalists like Laurent and Josie wrote eloquently about the bravery of the Czechoslovaks, telling stories that would resonate and inspire people around the world for years. At the time, no one was able to prove that a small coterie of Czechoslovak officials had betrayed their country by inviting an invasion.

Decades later, however, it was revealed that the letter to Eastern bloc newspapers, which Laurent reports on, had indeed been written by such a group, a collection of hard-liners opposed to the reforms of the Prague Spring. They had also planned a coup d'etat, but abandoned it in the hours before the invasion.

From the Author

As a reader, you make a book come alive. Thank you!

If you enjoyed *Strawberry Fields*, check out *Back in the USSR*, the next book in my Sing & Shout series. You'll meet Prudence, Josie and Laurent's fearless daughter, and her friend Harrison, the daydreaming son of American diplomats, on a thrilling mission to find a lost Beatles record in Cold War Moscow.

To hear about new releases and receive a free short story, sign up for my author updates at patrickdjoyce.com.

And if you have a moment, please leave a quick review of *Strawberry Fields* online. Sharing your thoughts helps new readers discover the book!

About the Author

I write historical thriller novels that combine mystery and suspense with a powerful sense of place.

As the son of a U.S. Foreign Service officer, I grew up in extraordinary places. After early years in Burma (Myanmar), West Germany, and Washington, D.C., I lived in Nicaragua, Cuba, and three times in the Soviet Union. At embassies staffed by diplomats, Marines, and spies, I was surrounded by secrets.

In addition to writing books, I've been a newspaper reporter, a political science lecturer, and a medical practice manager. I live in Massachusetts, where I can be found haunting coffee shops, taking long walks with my wife, and practicing martial arts.

Acknowledgments

My sincerest thanks go to Obadiah Jones, Barbara Katzenberg, and Klara Velicka for their thoughtful feedback on drafts of this book; to Karen Krumpak for her meticulous editing; to the team at Damonza for a stunning cover design; and to Rajee, Arjun, and Priya for their insight, love, and assistance on pretty much everything.

9 798986 169941